S0-BLY-898

This Book belongs to...
©A.K.Rush '84
and anybody who is Friendly with Bears can find it." --A. A. Milne, THE HOUSE AT POOH CORNER
"The Forest will always be there . . .

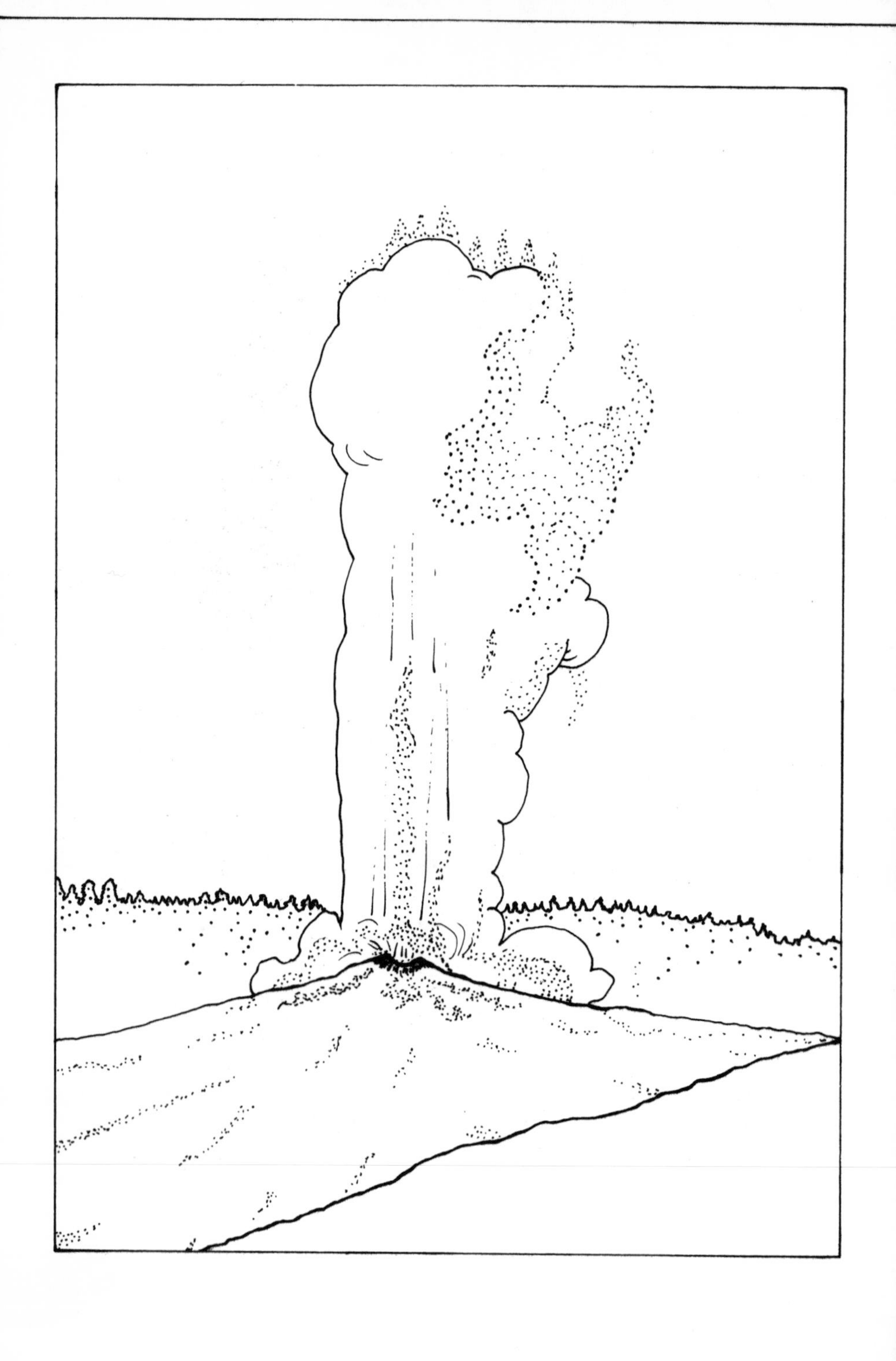

GRETA BEAR GOES TO YELLOWSTONE NATIONAL PARK

Anne Kent Rush

Greta Bear Enterprizes

This book is dedicated to
the adventurous, peaceful Bear Spirit
and to Everyone who shares it

First Edition, Spring, 1984, A GRETA BEAR™ Product.
Greta Bear Enterprizes, Post Office Box 9525, Berkeley, California 94709, U.S.A.

Individual copies of this book may be ordered from the publisher for $5.95 plus $1.50 for postage and handling. (For catalog and Friends of Bears information, see last page.)

Trade and library orders can be placed through many book distributors, including BOOK PEOPLE, 2929 Fifth Street, Berkeley, California 94710.

84-80077
Library of Congress Cataloging in Publication Data
Rush, Anne Kent, 1945

Greta Bear goes to Yellowstone National Park

1 I

RD
ISBN 0-931452-02-3 Paperback
ISBN 0-931452-01-5 Cloth

Manufactured in the U.S.A.

CONTENTS

On a famous trip to the wilderness in 1902 President Theodore Roosevelt refused to shoot a bear cub. When a cartoon about the incident appeared in newspapers, a company named some of their toys after Theodore. The "Teddy Bear" was born carrying, along with playfulness, a special association with care for wild creatures and places. Taking their heritage to heart, Teddy Bears have continued their work of bringing us closer to real bears in the most affectionate ways.

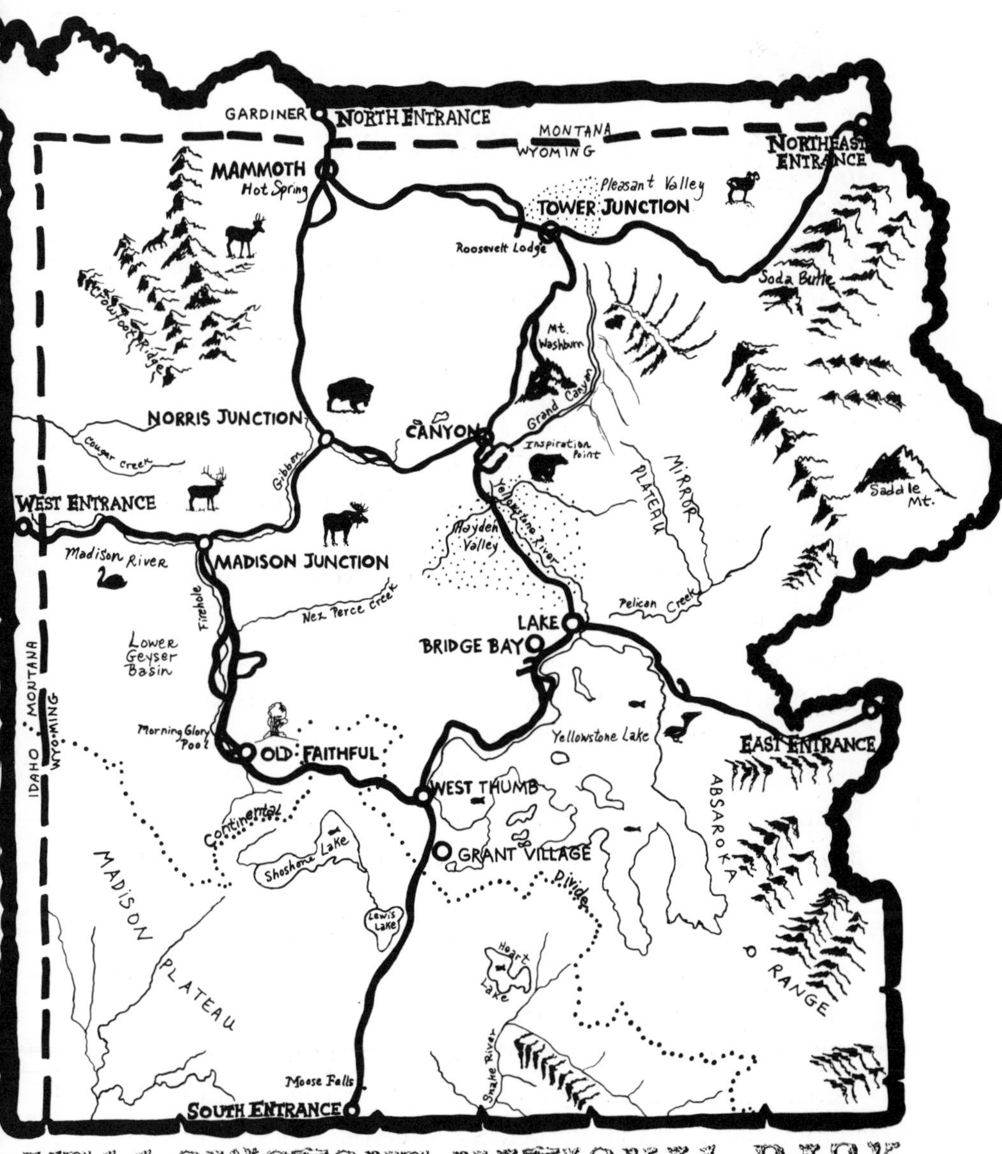
GARDINER
NORTH ENTRANCE
MONTANA
WYOMING
NORTHEAST ENTRANCE
MAMMOTH
Hot Spring
Pleasant Valley
TOWER JUNCTION
Roosevelt Lodge
Soda Butte
Crowfoot Ridge
Mt. Washburn
Grand Canyon
NORRIS JUNCTION
CANYON
Inspiration Point
Cougar Creek
Gibbon
MIRROR
PLATEAU
Saddle Mt.
WEST ENTRANCE
Yellowstone River
Hayden Valley
Madison River
MADISON JUNCTION
Firehole
Nez Perce Creek
Pelican Creek
LAKE
BRIDGE BAY
Lower Geyser Basin
IDAHO
MONTANA
WYOMING
Morning Glory Pool
OLD FAITHFUL
Yellowstone Lake
EAST ENTRANCE
WEST THUMB
Continental
ABSAROKA
Shoshone Lake
GRANT VILLAGE
MADISON
Divide
Lewis Lake
Heart Lake
RANGE
PLATEAU
Snake River
Moose Falls
SOUTH ENTRANCE
YELLOWSTONE NATIONAL PARK

INTRODUCTION

This is the story of two friends in search of a frontier. Greta, a toy bear made in a city factory, has the call of the wild in her heart. Claire, the girl who chooses Greta Bear from the other toys on the shelf, is an experienced camper. The two enter one of the most extensive and wondrous wilderness areas in America today, Yellowstone National Park.

The two million acres of Wyoming, Montana and Idaho that make up Yellowstone National Park remain today what they have always been, the home of many species of wild animals, including buffalo, elk and bear as well as the site of countless natural wonders such as boiling geysers, waterfall-drenched canyons and snow-capped mountains. Within the boundaries of Yellowstone, Claire and Greta Bear discover adventure in the wilds of America and the magic of living in harmony with nature.

The story is a fantasy tale meant for many readings, and is part of a series in which the pair travel to other exciting places. This is also a practical guidebook to the park through which children can learn information about wild animals and safe outdoor living. If you and your family follow Claire and Greta Bear's route you will visit most of the popular spots in Yellowstone.

In vast, wild places such as Yellowstone people have the chance to share the terrain peacefully and equally with other creatures. With the establishment of a national park, we secure not only a beautiful area of the earth and the varied life forms it supports, but also an irreplaceable resource of the human spirit. We can experience that the "wild" in "wilderness" is not always there to be tamed, but whenever possible, enjoyed and let be. Frontiers are not meant to be eliminated, but to be learned from and explored again and again.

Jackson Hole, Wyoming
Thanksgiving 1980

1
THE BEAR SPIRIT

In the night sky there is a black bear whose body is rimmed with stars. Look up and you'll see her shimmering near the steady North Star. Three stars shape her bright shoulders and head. Eleven stars line her front and back paws. And her haunches out to the tip of her long tail are made of the seven stars of the Big Dipper. Each star touching her body has a different name: Benetnasch, Alcor, Mizar, Alioth, orange Megrez, yellow Phad, yellow Dubhe and green Merak.

These stars form the Great Bear Mother constellation called Ursa Major. Her life has been longer than we have told each other stories. She looks out at the universe as far as a star can see. Her cub, the Little Dipper or Ursa Minor, lives nearby with the North Star on his tail. On the 29 stars of the Big and Little Dippers live all the bear spirits of our galaxy. And they watch over the needs of bears and the friends of bears.

When Ursa Major looked down on earth, she saw that many people were cut off from the bear spirit. So she gave toy bears to the world to help keep the bear spirit alive in big cities. Ursa Major knew that many people had forgotten how to love the things a bear loves—trees, rivers, canyons, fish, honey, warm beds, freedom, hugs, play and the songs of birds and coyotes. Ursa chose Greta Bear,

The Great Bear and her cub, the Little Dipper

from the star Merak, to go to Earth on the Bear Quest to help save bears.

Greta Bear was told to find other earth inhabitants to join the Bear Quest. As she listened to her instructions from Ursa Major, Greta decided to look for help first among children. She knew human children were spirits much like bear cubs and many had not forgotten, as some adults had, that all creatures are one family in spirit. As a young bear spirit, Greta had the wisdom of children who love the earth and all her creatures. All things considered Ursa Major thought Greta was the right bear for the job.

Ursa Major taught Greta some secrets of the Bear Cult to use as magic if she needed it. She taught Greta Bear how to act in a world where few people believed a bear or any animal had a spirit. Ursa gave Greta a red backpack that unfolded into a flying cape. Ursa told Greta to check up with her at night time if she needed her. Most

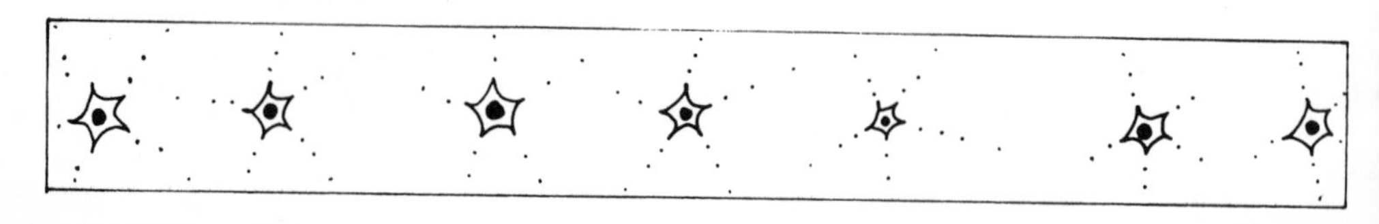

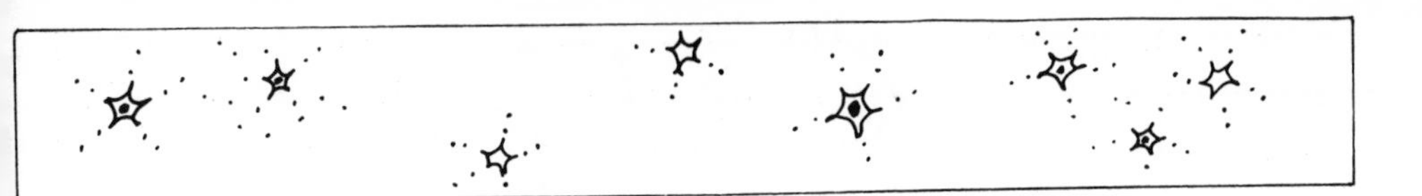

of all she encouraged Greta to be open to good spirits and to learn from everything around her. Ursa told Greta that on Earth the only really powerful magic was the power of the heart. She said Greta would come to understand this as she moved in the world. Ursa kissed the little bear seven times. Then Ursa and Greta hugged and exchanged the Bear Oath:

Through the bright day
We play with no cares
And roam with our hearts
In the spirit of the bear.

Through the dark night
We sleep with no fear
And dream with our hearts
In the spirit of the bear.

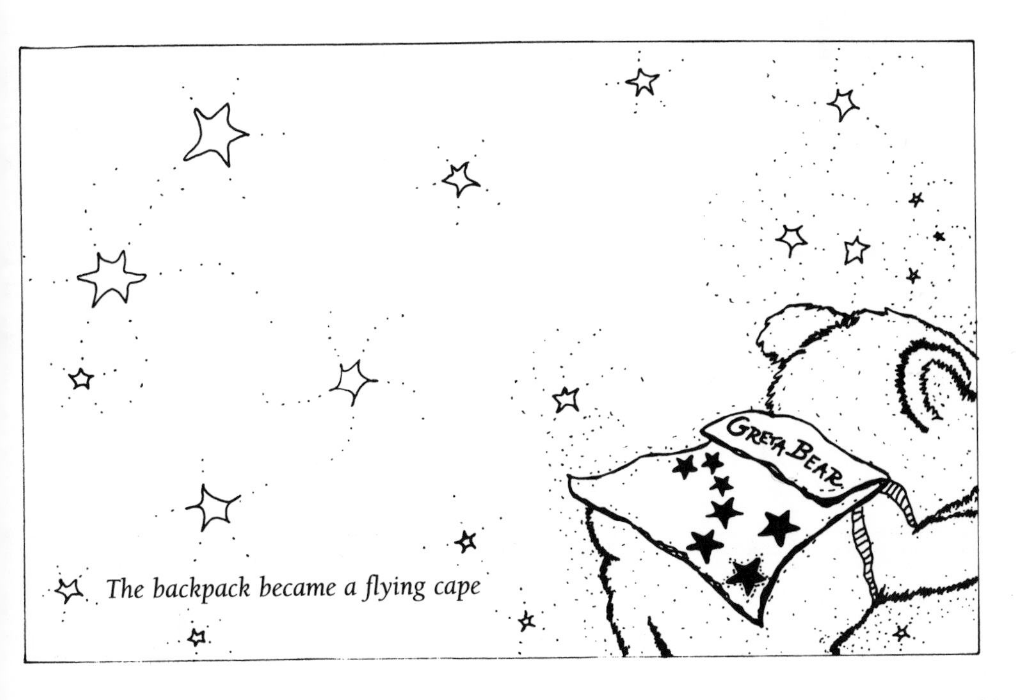

The backpack became a flying cape

Leaving Merak was hard for Greta. It was a beautiful place to live and full of shiny spirits. But she was excited to start her mission and go to a new place. She would meet new beings, have fresh adventures and perhaps meet some of earth's wild bears.

Greta Bear started her journey from Merak on the back of the winged horse, Pegasus. On and on they flew through the night past many stars and beings who sang the song of constant change.

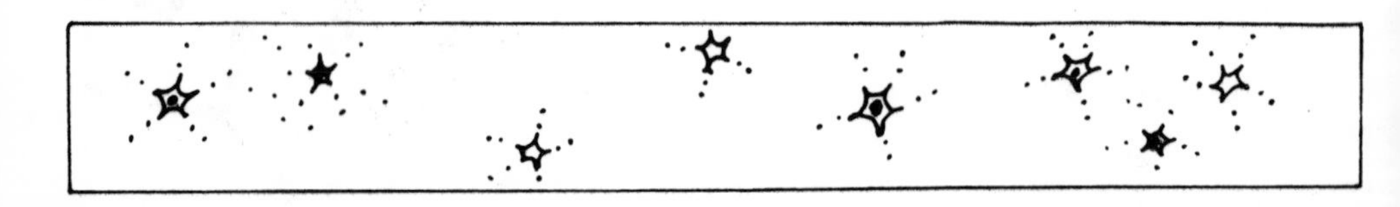

Greta Bear rode the winged horse

2
DREAMS OF ADVENTURE

After a fine, windy journey through the sky, the horse, Pegasus, and Greta Bear landed on Earth at a toy factory in San Francisco. Here Greta began her life as a city bear. Everything was new and exciting. She learned about crowds, cars, shops and streets.

She also heard about another kind of place, the country. Many city people spent weekends in the country, or the great outdoors, as they sometimes called it, and told stories about their experiences at work on Mondays.

The factory toy makers told about places called national parks where the animals were different from Greta and her friends. The animals looked like toys, but they were "wild." Wild meant that they roamed free; they lived as their ancestors had in the wilderness; and they did not know about playing with people. This interested Greta because the only creatures she'd met besides bear spirits had been people and toys.

Greta felt in her heart she was like the wild animals and she longed to visit them. During the day Greta read the addresses on the packages of toys ready for mailing and tried to guess what the far-off places on the labels were like. At night Greta snuggled against her new toy friend, the floppy moose. She imagined the concrete walls of the factory fading away until trees grew up in the

Trees grew up in the shadows of her dreams

shadows of her dreams.

One morning Greta heard the manager of the factory tell a truck driver, "Deliver these toys to Canyon Village Shop in Yellowstone National Park." The driver had been to the park in Wyoming before, and while he was packing some toys in a box he told the manager stories that made Yellowstone sound like a place full of adventure.

No one noticed Greta climb off the warehouse shelf and into the packing crate. The driver finished, shook hands with the manager and loaded the crate into the back of his truck. Greta heard the engine start and felt the truck turn onto the superhighway.

After a quiet life in the toy factory Greta was ready for a challenge. She daydreamed of what she might do in Yellowstone. She longed to explore a world of wild animals and natural wonders. When she was happy Greta Bear sometimes found songs coming out of her. She began singing to herself.

No one saw Greta climb into the crate

I'm a city bear with a country heart
And I'm on my way to a national park
I will roam like bears who live in the park
Where the great outdoors is my own backyard

The other stuffed animals liked her song and joined in the chorus:

Round 'em up, head 'em out
Giddy-up, let's go
Hey ho, let's go to a national park
Hey ho, let's go to a national park

Then Greta made up another verse:

There the air is clear and the sun is hot
There the trails are long and the shorts are short
I will hike the hills till the sky gets dark
Then I'll spend the night under sleepy stars

And all the toy animals sang with her:

Round 'em up, head 'em out
Giddy-up, let's go
Hey ho, let's go to a national park
Hey ho, let's go to a national park

After so much singing they were all tired. Greta Bear fell asleep to the humming of the truck's wheels.

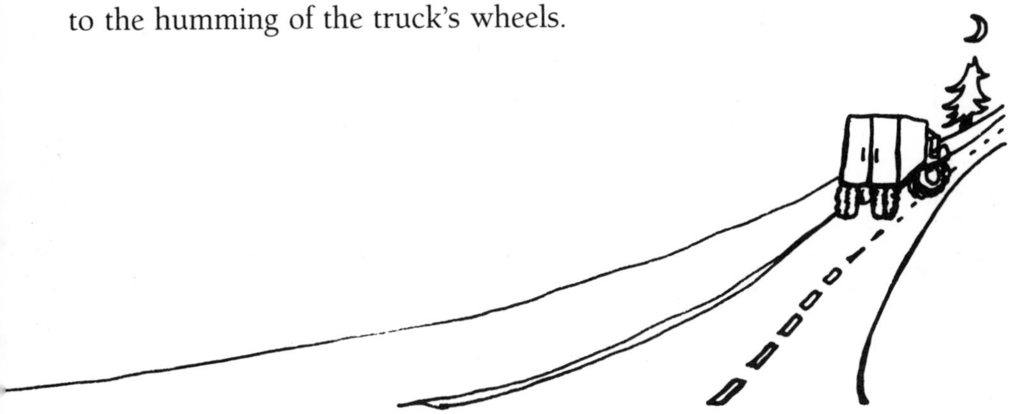

3
BEAR FOR SALE

Drowsy days went by as the truck made its way across western states. In the middle of a dream of napping in a meadow, Greta was awakened by the sound of the steel doors banging open, and the crate was lifted out of the truck. The driver walked across gravel, up some stairs and dropped the box on a concrete floor. Greta heard the driver leave.

All the toys were awake now and wondered what awaited them outside. They heard two women's voices discussing where to put them. A knife crunched into the cardboard. As the sides of the box opened, Greta could see sunlight streaming through a window.

The women took the toys from the box and placed them in different parts of the store. From her shelf Greta looked out past a display of cowboy hats. She saw rows of cars in a parking lot.

This doesn't look the way I imagined Yellowstone Park, she thought. How could a moose or a swan live in a parking lot?

One of the women said, "It's five o'clock. We finished unloading just in time."

The other woman said, "What beautiful new toys they are. They look so much like real animals!" Then the two women walked outside, locked the door and left the shop.

Yes, they were all fine toys, and Greta was proud to be herself, with dark brown fur, strong legs, soft paws and a good bear brain. The red camper's pack on her back made her feel ready for adventure with the creatures of the wilderness and all their friends.

Now though when she looked at her usually crisp backpack she could see that it was rumpled from the tight squeeze in the crate and her fur was rather messy. Greta looked around at the other animals. They were busy licking, paw-combing and generally tidying up for the next morning in the store. Greta began brushing her fur.

Next to her the moose was complaining about the heat and scraping his felt horns along the posts at the end of the shelf. "I wanted to come to Yellowstone," the moose said, "because everybody talked about the ponds and marshes. Everyone knows a moose loves wading knee-deep in marshes and eating the delicious grasses that grow there. At least, that's what I've heard a wild moose loves. And I want to try it. I hope a customer who loves ponds picks me. But, you know, Greta, even if we don't get picked I like it here okay. I like being your friend. And really I'm not so sure I'll love getting wet!"

Greta stayed up late that night

"I like being your friend too," said Greta.

"Maybe the same person will pick us," he said. "And we could go on an adventure together." Thinking of adventures made the moose rather tired so he closed his eyes to dream of green marshes.

Greta, however, was wide awake and she had something special in mind. She climbed down from her shelf over to the book section of the store. A long time after the other toys were asleep Greta stayed up reading as many books as she could about animals and plants in Yellowstone. She learned much information that made her feel well prepared for a new life in the great outdoors. Finally Greta began to feel awfully sleepy. She climbed back onto her shelf to lie down beside the floppy moose. The last thing she saw before her eyes closed was a sign over the door that read like a dream come true, "Canyon Village, Yellowstone National Park."

The toys slept so soundly that they only woke up when they heard a key turning in the lock. The saleswomen came inside and left the door ajar. Greta could smell the fresh morning air and feel the sunlight. After a good night's sleep all the toys were at their best, and each tried to look like the perfect toy to take home. Many customers came through the store asking for souvenirs, but no one seemed to look at Greta.

Greta was about to abandon hope of ever seeing the park, when a tall young man with sandy hair and blue eyes walked up to her shelf. Greta straightened her pack and stretched out her front paws.

"She's terrific!" said Claire

"What do you think of this bear, Claire?" the man said. "The tag says her name is Greta." He picked up Greta and handed her to a girl about nine years old with brown eyes and big curls.

"She's terrific!" said Claire. "She has a backpack too and looks ready to explore Yellowstone with me."

It pays to be ready for adventure, thought Greta, who could hardly keep from giving Claire a warm bear hug, but she was careful to keep still. Claire carried Greta Bear out of the store. Now I'm on my way, she thought; I'm on my way to the great outdoors!

"I'm on my way!"

4
A NEW LIFE IN THE GREAT OUTDOORS

Claire gave Greta a kiss and said, "This bear is just the right size to fit in my backpack." Claire also picked out a drawing pad and paid the saleswoman with part of her allowance. "I want to keep a diary of my trip and draw the plants and animals I see," said Claire. She put the notebook in her pack and fit Greta snugly into the outside pocket.

An adventurous location, thought Greta, I can see quite well from here.

"Jake," said one of the saleswomen, "who's your new friend?"

"Pat, this is my younger sister, Claire." Jake put his arm around Claire's shoulders and gave her a squeeze. Claire beamed proudly.

"Well, the two of you should have a fine time in the park," said Pat. "What animals are you photographing this time?"

"On this trip I'm particularly interested in elk," said Jake. "But we'll try to see as much as we can of Yellowstone because this is Claire's first visit. We'll take one of the popular tourist routes to see many different animals and geysers. We don't get out here from the city very often." Jake bought several rolls of film and a park guidebook for Claire.

He picked a good one, Greta thought, remembering the pictures she had seen in it the night before.

Then Jake said to Claire, "Well, my friend, it's time to go if we want to get an early start."

"Do we have to go now?" asked Claire who was busy looking at a book on the wildflowers of Yellowstone.

"Does a bear sleep in the woods?" asked Jake.

"Jake," said Claire, "I want to stay longer."

"Well, does he?" said Jake.

"Of course," answered Claire.

"Then let's go!" exclaimed Jake.

"Goodbye. Have a good time!" said the saleswoman laughing.

They walked out into the sunlight, then climbed into a white van, and Jake started the engine.

Jake and Claire are pleasant names for friends, Greta thought, but are they the names of great adventurers? I hope so.

Claire took off her pack and put it on the front seat. "Greta, you can look out the window from here," said Claire.

"Are you talking to that toy?" said Jake.

"Of course," answered Claire. "It may take a little time, but after a while toys can understand you, didn't you know?"

"I learn something new every day!" said Jake.

They walked out into the sunlight

Hmm, Claire knows something about magic, thought Greta. Looking out the window, Greta was encouraged that beyond the parking lot she could see a pine forest and beyond that the peaks of blue mountains. Greta's heart soared. If wild animals live anywhere, she thought, they must live here.

Jake drove the van down a road that wound through fields of golden grass threaded with rivers and forests. Greta had never seen so much land without houses on it or such long roads without billboards. As she gazed at the meadows and the endless view of hills, a sense of peacefulness came over her. She was feeling happy that she could make wishes come true when she tried. After all, a few days ago, she had been in San Francisco dreaming of wilderness. Now here she was in Yellowstone!

Greta knew many challenges lay ahead. Many things would happen that would test her strength and knowledge, but her preparation from Ursa Major made her confident. As she looked out of the window she began singing softly.

Greta was so excited that she forgot that most people might be surprised to see a toy bear singing, but Jake and Claire didn't seem to notice and the song made Greta Bear feel very good.

With my soft brown nose
And my small round ears
And my pack snug under my chin
I'm a bear that's ready for adventure
I'm a bear that's ready to begin!

Although I've come from the city
And was raised as a city child
My heart belongs to the great outdoors
Where the trees and bears grow wild!

Give me a good strong pack
And some sturdy boots
And a pair of country jeans
I'm a bear that's ready to climb mountains
I'm a bear that's ready to fish streams!

I'm a bear that's ready for adventure!
I'm a city bear ready to be wild!
I'm a city bear ready for the country!
I'm a city bear ready to be wild!
I'm a city bear ready
I'm a city bear ready
I'm a city bear ready to be wild!

5
A BUFFALO ROAMING

After awhile Jake stopped the van. "It's time for a snack. Let's break out the nuts and orange juice."

As Claire and Jake were preparing their food, Greta saw something large out the window she had never seen before. It had darker brown fur than Greta's, and legs that ended in gray stumps that looked like stones. It had a neck with a big hump on top and its head had small dark eyes over which grew large horns.

Then it took several steps forward. Greta jumped up in surprise. It put its head down and munched on the yellow grass. Greta felt fairly safe behind the window of the van. But she wasn't sure what the animal would do next. What does it like to eat besides grass? Surely not bears, she thought. What will I do if it runs toward the van? Can I talk with it? Greta understood her toy animal friends because they were just like her, but this was a new situation.

This must be what the factory workers meant when they described the excitement of meeting a wild animal. I guess "wild" means not knowing what something will do next. Hmm, thought Greta, this feels different than I expected. But at least the books I read prepared me to recognize it. I know from a picture in the guidebook that this is a buffalo, a large buffalo.

Greta saw something large with horns

Greta thought that one difference between city bears and country bears must be that country bears knew about wilderness living without having to read a guidebook. But city bears can learn, she thought. And it's a good thing I studied about the animals because Claire and Jake might not be with me all the time. What if I had been alone in the field with this buffalo? Her paws shaking a bit, Greta leaned forward in the pack for a better look at the animal. She thought about what the guidebook had said about buffalo.

> Bison, sometimes called buffalo. Up to 6 feet tall, hoofed adults can weigh as much as 2,000 pounds. Shaggy hair on shoulders and front legs. Buffalo calves are born in May or June. They live in meadows or forests and eat grass and sedge. Fond of wallowing in the dust. May attack an animal that threatens their young. Since most buffalo were killed by early Americans and settlers, Yellowstone Park is one of the last homelands of the buffalo.

"Hey, Jake, what's big, has a horn and runs in Yellowstone?" said Claire.

"A camper truck," said Jake.

"No, that buffalo over there."

"Terrific! I want to photograph it!" Jake said as he took out his camera.

Greta felt proud to have seen the buffalo and figured out what it was. Claire was drawing a picture in her notebook of a buffalo grazing. I'm glad the buffalo have a home in Yellowstone, Greta thought.

After taking some photographs Jake said, "Let's go. We have a lot more to see today!"

Yellowstone is one of the last homelands of the buffalo

6

GEYSERS, HOTSPRINGS AND MUD POTS

As they drove down the road the sight of the buffalo grew smaller. Jake turned off the main stretch and the road wound awhile through pine forest. Passing a river Greta saw a sign that read, "Gibbon River," and another, "Virginia Cascades." She was wondering what a cascade was when she saw the river water begin to tumble over itself. Bubbling down the steep rocks it tossed up white foam and made a pleasant, gurgling sound. Greta decided she liked cascades very much.

When they turned back onto the main road, the scenery changed. The grass grew shorter and the ground was yellow and cracked. Greta saw something mysterious rising up from a small pool in the earth. It was white moving water and the curly top of it knew how to ride on the air, while the bottom danced and bubbled. Greta saw a sign which read, "Norris Geyser Basin," and realized this must be one of the natural fountains and pools of hot water the people back in San Francisco had talked about. She felt quite knowledgeable and wished her friend, the floppy moose, were there to talk to. When she thought about the floppy moose she missed him and hoped she would see him again. But she was more excited than lonely now because she was seeing all the interesting things she had read about.

Explanation of Hydrothermal Features: Hydro means water and thermal means heat. If water is heated by hot rock deep in the earth, it can create a hot spring or geyser. A hot spring is a pool of hot water. A geyser is a pool which sometimes jets into the air like a fountain. If the water heats the mud until it bubbles, it's called a mud pot. Plants, bacteria or minerals in the area can turn the pools unusual colors. Yellowstone Park has more hot springs and geysers in one area than any other place in the world.

Driving along they saw many clouds of steam rising in the air. There seemed to be hundreds of hot pools. People were moving around the edges on wooden walkways. These were built by the Park Service so that no one would get burned by hot water or fall into the sticky mud. Greta saw signs that read, "Porcelain Basin," "Little Whirligig," "Blue Geyser," "Whale's Mouth," "Fireball." These names told Greta something about each spring.

The hot pools looked inviting to Greta. I wonder if you can sit in them like a warm bath. People say warm baths feel good.

"Claire, would you like to get out to look at this hot spring?" said Jake.

"Does a bear sleep in the woods?" said Claire.

Jake laughed, parked the van, and they climbed out. Claire carried Greta in her backpack.

Bubbling Mud Pots

They stood by the pool and Greta gazed at the lovely, clear water. As Claire turned around to head for the van Greta leaned forward in her pocket for a last look. Claire stumbled a bit on the dry earth and Greta was thrown out of the pack. I'm a bear made for adventure, she thought, and here goes! She fell into the hot spring with a splash.

Ouch! This is too hot! It's not as pleasant to sit in as to look at, Greta thought. Then she realized she was sinking!

Claire heard the splash and turned around just as Greta's nose was disappearing below the green water. Luckily a ranger on a horse nearby had seen Greta fall. He jumped off his horse, rushed over and dragged Greta to the side of the pool with a branch. He handed a wet Greta to Claire.

"It's a good thing this was just a stuffed bear," the ranger said. "If it had been a person, their skin would have been badly burned."

"Greta," exclaimed Claire, "what a terrible fall you've taken. I'm so glad you didn't sink. Now we'll have to dry you out in the sun. And thank you, ranger, for saving my bear."

"My name's Hawk," said the ranger. "Come say hello next time you and your bear are in the area."

Well, thought Greta, I'll take park warnings more seriously from now on and not lean over hot springs. Things here are not so safe as they are on Merak, and the warnings are here to protect me. I want to be a smart adventurer. And danger is different from adventure.

Claire and Jake sat on some big rocks in the sun while Greta was drying out. Hawk, the park ranger, gave them suggestions about where to go to see wild animals. By the time they drove down the road again, Greta felt she was a more country-wise bear for her experience.

"Ouch! This is too hot!"

7
GRETA MEETS A COUNTRY MOOSE

Greta, Claire and Jake drove on through the park as the sky was turning lavender and the afternoon air was cooling. Time for all bears to take a nap, Greta thought. As she was snuggling into Claire's pack, out the window Greta saw an unusual brown shape walking into a stream. It looked a little bit like the buffalo, but skinnier and the horns on its head were bigger. She remembered reading the chapter in the guidebook that described a wild moose.

> Moose. Largest relative of the deer. Stands about 6 feet high and can weigh up to 1,400 pounds. Dark brown to black fur. Has a beard under its chin called a "dewlap." Has large ears, long nose and hooves. Eats mainly willow leaves and water plants, including water lilies. Often travels alone unless with calves. Mothers will charge those who threaten their young. Usually has poor vision, good hearing and a good sense of smell. Can live well in the deep snow in winter.

Greta thought of her friend, the city moose, and wished he could see this magnificent wild animal. Jake saw it too and stopped the car. He and Claire got out and started walking across the field.

The moose kept munching the water grass

Greta thought the situation over for a moment. It made her nervous to think of leaving the car. At the same time it upset her to think of not meeting the moose. Here I am at last, free in the wide open spaces where I've wanted to be. How can I miss my chance for adventure? Besides, it says in the guidebook that if you keep your distance moose aren't annoyed unless they have calves. Greta looked around the field for a sign of a calf, but there was just one enormous moose eating weeds.

Greta flexed her legs and ruffled her fur, generally getting into physical shape for the field trip. The van window was open so she could climb easily to the ground. A song can be helpful at times for making you brave, she thought. As she put one furry foot out the window, she began singing:

When I see a moose
That is free and loose
I most naturally want to meet it
I approach with care
And stop halfway there
That's the politest way to greet it!

When Greta slid to the ground she saw that Jake and Claire were sitting on the bank of the stream. Claire was drawing in her notebook. The moose gave them an occasional glance and kept munching the water grass, swaying its head from side to side. Jake and Claire were watching the moose so intently that they didn't notice when Greta sat down near them. The sunset had turned the sky tangerine color behind the moose, whose swaying motion made Greta feel calm.

They sat quietly watching the moose

Jake took some photographs and Claire finished her sketch. They stayed quietly watching the moose while the sky melted into deep blue and the air became chilly. Then they got up together. Walking toward the car, Greta thought how good it felt to sit with the moose. When they reached the truck and Jake opened the door, Greta scrambled quickly onto the seat before anyone noticed her. Back in the van Greta thought how sometimes adventure happens when you are moving fast, and sometimes adventure happens when you are still. The three of them drove down the road in the starry twilight toward a new adventure.

8
A CAMPGROUND IN THE STARLIGHT

Greta began to feel hungry. Eating is one of the things that bears particularly like to do. I wonder when Jake and Claire will feed me? Actually, Greta thought, being free in the great outdoors also includes learning to find my own food. Let's see what there is to eat in this pack.

Greta wriggled down into the pack and poked around. I hope my companions have good taste in food, she thought. That's important when you are on adventures together. Greta found some yellow cubes in a plastic bag. Cheese, she thought. I don't think bears like cheese. The next parcel looked more promising. It was a package of brown bread. And in the corner of the pack she could see a small honey jar. Bread with honey is a fine dinner for a camping bear. Greta made herself some sandwiches which she ate very fast. Then she licked her paws and nose for the last sticky drops.

Climbing out of the pack Greta saw that the road was heading into a forest. They drove until they saw some lights. As the van rounded a turn, a sign appeared that read, "National Park Campground." Jake drove past the sign and up to a log cabin. On the shelf was a stack of papers. Jake took out a pen and wrote awhile; then he took some money out of his pocket and sealed it in an envelope. Greta knew from conversations of the toy factory workers that campers had to pay the National Park Service a small amount to stay overnight in a park campground. He dropped the envelope in a slot above the shelf.

Bread with honey for dinner

Jake got back in the van and drove down a dirt road. On either side of the road were cars and people gathered around campfires. Some were eating on picnic tables. Others already turned in for the night were curled up inside their tents or tucked in their camper trucks fast asleep. Jake found an open parking area and pulled his car into the space.

"Time for dinner," Jake said.

It was time for my dinner a long time ago, Greta thought.

Jake reached inside his pack and pulled out a bag of cheese and a loaf of bread. Then he poured some water from a thermos into a pan and heated it with some tea leaves on a small electric stove in the back of his truck. When Jake turned a light on in his truck, Greta could see that there was a mattress with sheets and pillows in the back, and two fluffy down sleeping bags on top. Greta had been wondering where she would spend the night and was relieved that Jake had such a comfortable-looking bed.

Jake and Claire finished their dinner and put away the cooking equipment.

"Let's sleep outside tonight," said Jake, "so we can breathe the fresh air and see the stars overhead."

"Oh good," thought Greta, "that's even better. My first night out will be really outdoors!"

Jake found an area free of bushes and stones and spread a waterproof ground cloth over a level place padded with pine needles. Claire and Jake put up the tent and then put the two sleeping bags on the ground cloth. They hung their food supplies high on ropes strung from trees so the forest bears wouldn't come for it to the campground.

Then they took off their sweaters and jeans, climbed into the sleeping bags and lay with their heads at the opening of the tent. Claire put Greta under the soft edge of her down bag, and Jake and Claire fell asleep.

Greta was wide awake. She enjoyed looking out at the campfires burning in the dark. Up in the sky she could see the stars twinkling. So many more stars seemed to shimmer above Yellowstone than above the big city! She had heard the factory workers talk about how smoke from cars and industries clouded the city skies so that it was hard for people to breathe well or see stars anymore. Greta couldn't imagine why people loved smoke more than stars. She decided to take a walk in the moonlight to get a better look at her home star in the Big Dipper.

Greta saw Ursa Major twinkling in the sky

9
GRETA HELPS PREVENT A FOREST FIRE

In the night stillness, the only sound Greta heard was an owl's low hoot. She crawled out from under Claire's sleeping bag and headed toward the woods. The trees seemed to be different creatures in the moonlight than in the sun of day. Their trunks looked taller and their leaves looked blue and silver. She made up a song as she walked:

At last it's night time,
The moon is shining.

The stars are blinking
Because they're sleepy.

The owls are hooting
While out cahooting.

Coyotes keep yawning
While bears are snoring.

It may be dark out
But it's not boring.

Then Greta noticed something unusual—a glowing patch on the ground several feet ahead of her. She went over to investigate and discovered a small pile of pine needles burning red. Most people in the campsite had

carefully put out their campfires by pouring water over the last sparks so the embers were cold and smokeless. But someone had carelessly tossed a cigarette which was still burning into the leaves. As Greta watched, the red spot grew and lit up more leaves.

I've got to do something quickly, Greta thought, or this could become a big fire and burn down the whole forest! She had read about fires in the guidebook and remembered sometimes you could smother them with earth. Greta began furiously digging up dirt with her paws and kicking it onto the red pine needles. After a few minutes hard work the glow grew smaller in some places but still burned in others.

Then she remembered that the book said the best thing to do on seeing a fire in a national park was to call a ranger. But how could she do that? She ran back to the tent and tugged at Claire's sleeping bag to try to wake her. Then she boxed Claire's nose a little. Claire sat up, eyed Greta suspiciously and looked around. Then she saw the fire starting in the dark. Claire grabbed her bluejeans and sweater and woke up Jake.

"There's a fire starting! Wake up the other campers! I'm going to get the ranger!" She ran to the ranger station and knocked loudly. When the ranger opened the door, Claire said, "A fire's starting near my tent!"

The ranger grabbed a fire extinguisher and followed Claire. She showed him the spot and he quickly put out the fire. Greta was pleased she had remembered the information from her guidebook, had acted quickly and had helped stop what could have been a terrible forest fire. Exhausted, she and Claire climbed back into the warm sleeping bag.

As her eyes were closing Greta Bear saw a bright streak in the sky sprinkle down from a paw of Ursa Major toward the tree tops. A falling star! What a day, she thought, a day full of adventure.

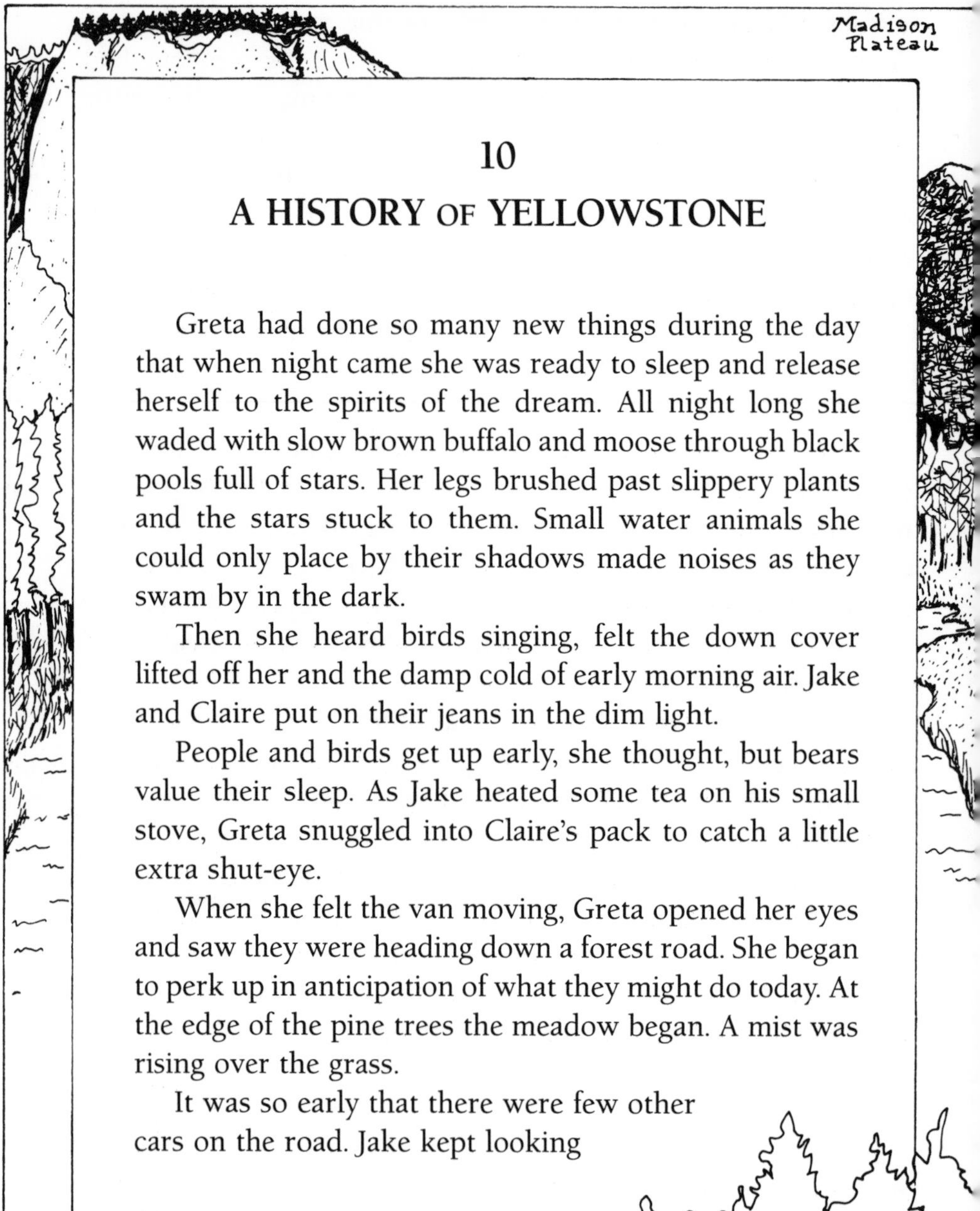

Madison Plateau

10
A HISTORY OF YELLOWSTONE

Greta had done so many new things during the day that when night came she was ready to sleep and release herself to the spirits of the dream. All night long she waded with slow brown buffalo and moose through black pools full of stars. Her legs brushed past slippery plants and the stars stuck to them. Small water animals she could only place by their shadows made noises as they swam by in the dark.

Then she heard birds singing, felt the down cover lifted off her and the damp cold of early morning air. Jake and Claire put on their jeans in the dim light.

People and birds get up early, she thought, but bears value their sleep. As Jake heated some tea on his small stove, Greta snuggled into Claire's pack to catch a little extra shut-eye.

When she felt the van moving, Greta opened her eyes and saw they were heading down a forest road. She began to perk up in anticipation of what they might do today. At the edge of the pine trees the meadow began. A mist was rising over the grass.

It was so early that there were few other cars on the road. Jake kept looking

The Hayden Expedition, 1871

intently into the trees on either side. Greta saw a sign that read, "Approaching Madison Junction."

"Would you like to read what the guidebook says about this area?" Jake said to Claire.

Claire turned to the section on Madison Junction, and said, "Listen to this, Greta."

> Driving from Norris Junction to Madison Junction you will pass an overlook on the roadside. Be sure to get out of your car and view Gibbon Falls, one of the loveliest waterfalls in the park.
>
> As you turn south on the Grand Loop Road you will see National Park Mountain, an extension of Madison Plateau, on your right. This is the famous spot where the explorers, Washburn, Langford and Doane, camped in 1870. They liked the area so much they decided to try to get the President of the U.S. to designate Yellowstone as a protected and undeveloped area. This effort was the beginning of saving national parks to preserve animals and forests. Except for limited areas where roads, restaurants and shops have been built to accommodate visitors, Yellowstone is still two million acres of untouched wilderness.

Long ago many tribes of Indians—Shoshoni, Blackfeet, Sioux, Plains—came through the area to hunt and camp. Then fur trappers came for beaver and bison. In the early 1800's the exploration party of Lewis and Clark allowed one of their members, John Colter, to cross Yellowstone on his own. Colter was one of the first white men to report to outsiders about the magnificent place. When Colter first told people about streams that spouted hot water and canyons made of yellow rock, no one believed him. Today people come to see for themselves. But we must remember that Yellowstone is mainly the home of the wild animals which have always lived here, and we should be careful not to interfere with the balance of nature. Or we must restore it if we destroy it.

As you drive on past Madison Plateau, you can follow a road that goes along the Firehole River and see Firehole Canyon with its walls of black rock. You can also see forty foot Firehole Falls. Most of the trees in this area are lodgepole pines. Indians used their tall trunks for poles in teepees and lodges. And many geysers dot this area in Lower Geyser Basin.

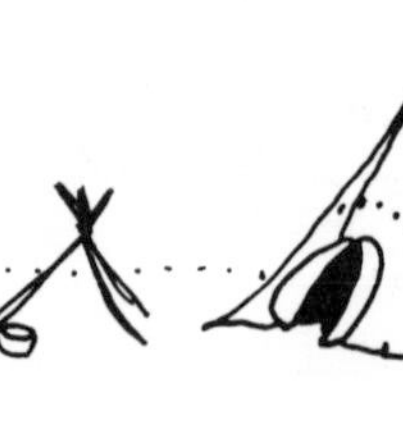

"The area has an interesting history, doesn't it, Greta?" asked Claire.

Interesting, thought Greta, but long. As Greta turned around to look out the window she saw something else which interested her. Next to the road moving uphill toward the trees were several large animals. They looked a little like the moose Greta had seen yesterday, but they were thinner and had tan fur on their rear ends and short tails.

Jake saw them too and exclaimed, "I knew there would be elk out here this time of morning!"

11
STALKING THE WILD ELK

Greta remembered a picture of an elk in the guidebook and under it had been the word, "wapiti," the Indian name for elk. The book had said that female elk did not have horns, or "antlers," as they were called. The elk Greta saw now must be male because they had huge, branching antlers just like in the pictures in her book.

Elk stand up to 5 feet high and may weigh as much as 1,000 pounds. The females will charge something that threatens their calves. The babies have spotted coats. Elk live in mountain meadows and forests. They eat grass and shrubs—aspen, serviceberry, snowbrush and bunchgrass are favorites. Females travel in groups called herds with their young. In late summer the furry coating on the male's antlers is rubbed off when the antlers have stopped growing. Then the males prepare for the mating season. In late winter or early spring their antlers will fall off altogether, but they grow back each summer. Most elk live at high altitudes in summer, but when the weather gets cold they travel to lower, warmer places. Many elk spend the winter around Jackson Hole.

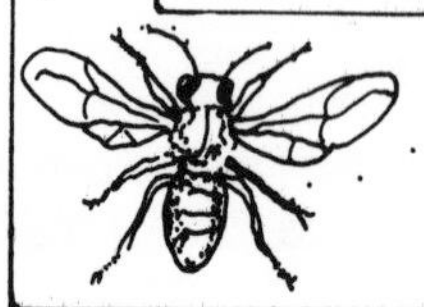

The elk munched their way across the meadow

Jake stopped the van and was rummaging around looking for his camera. Uh oh, Greta thought, he's going to get out there with the elk. Well, we were safe yesterday when we stayed at a good distance from the moose. Probably elk will let us watch them too.

Claire and Jake got out of the van and began climbing the hill behind the elk, with Greta in the pocket of Claire's backpack. They followed the two elk a long time in silence. The elk walked down the far side of the hill into a grassy meadow where they stopped to graze.

"What do you say when you meet two elk?" Claire whispered to Jake.

"Nothing," said Jake.

"Hello, hello," said Claire.

"Claire, elk like quiet better than jokes," Jake said.

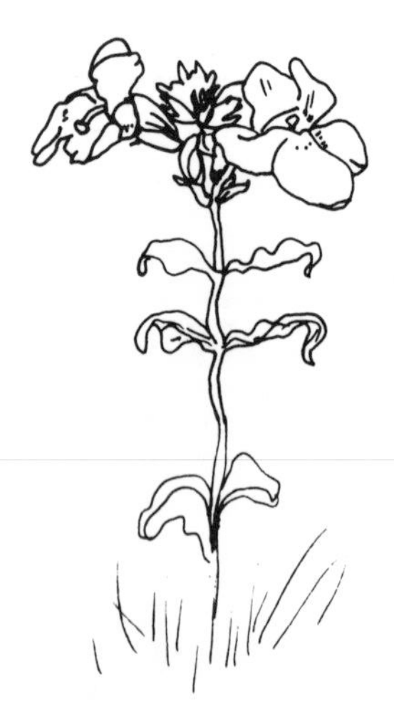

Yellow Monkey

Yarrow *Harebell*

The gray morning sky was slowly turning yellow as the sun rose. Greta could see down the hill far into the distance across a long valley. Claire put the pack down in the meadow. The fields were covered with wildflowers and sage brush which had a sweet smell that made Greta glad to breathe.

The pictures of wildflowers in the guidebook had names like Yellow Monkey, Yarrow, Harebell, Stonecrop, Blueflax, Indian Paintbrush, White Fringed Gentian. Greta thought about the name, "wildflowers." It must mean they can grow on their own, she thought, without needing people to plant or water them. She knew some plants had seeds that could be blown long distances on the wind and new ones could grow where the wind dropped the seeds. Greta lay down in the field gazing at the many colors and listening to the buzzing of the bees.

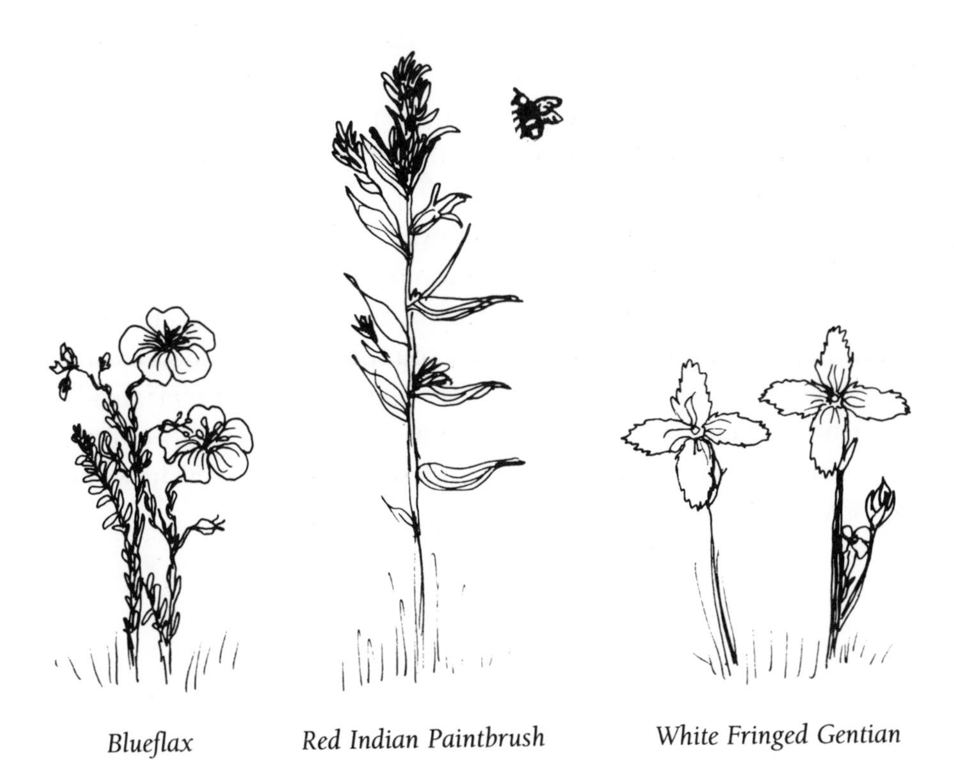

Blueflax *Red Indian Paintbrush* *White Fringed Gentian*

Today Greta was feeling more comfortable in an open field than she had the day before. She knew that unless something unusual startled the animals or she went too close to them, all of them could exist together peacefully. She began humming a song:

Some elk have hooves
And horns with fur,
But if an elk has hooves
And no antler
It's how you tell
A him from her.

Watching the two elk chew on the tall grass Greta thought, breakfast time is prime time to spend with elk. Thinking of breakfast reminded Greta that she hadn't had any. She looked over at Jake who was taking photographs of the animals from different angles. Maybe if he keeps watching the elk he will remember breakfast too. The elk kept grazing in the meadow, moving their heads slowly from side to side, lifting their big antlers now and then to see if Jake and Claire were still keeping their distance. Claire was drawing in her sketchbook. The elk made their way across the meadow to the foot of another hill. By this time the sun was high in the sky and the air was warm. The elk wandered up the hill and into a pine forest.

Jake, Claire and Greta Bear followed them. Among the trees when the elk stood still their antlers looked like branches, and they were so quiet you might walk right past them. Occasionally one would step on a branch and the crack sounded loud in the forest air. They watched them from behind a tree as the elk tilted their heads down and began slowly scraping their antlers on the trunks of pine trees. Greta remembered from the guidebook that this was how the elk took off the antlers' coating, called "velvet."

Then the elk found places where they could lie down comfortably on the forest floor. Here they would stay until the hottest part of the day was over. In the cool afternoon they might emerge from the forest to play by a stream or graze again. Jake, Claire and Greta turned away from the sleeping elk and headed back to the road.

"Hey, Jake, what goes zzub, zzub?" asked Claire.

"I don't know. I've never heard that sound," said Jake.

"A bee flying backward!" said Claire.

"Claire, you've heard of bees in your bonnet, haven't you?"

"Sure."

"Well, my friend, you've got 'em!" Jake exclaimed, and he raced Claire back to the van.

The elk lay down on the pine needles

12
CLAWS

While walking toward the roadway Greta noticed a bird that she had only seen before in pictures flying above her. She stopped to watch it as Claire and Jake walked on. The way the large bird was soaring interested Greta. It made wide circles in the air, floating for long periods without flapping its wings. She could see it had reddish brown tipped feathers and a lovely white belly. Greta recognized it as a red-tailed hawk.

Then Greta noticed that Claire and Jake had gotten far ahead of her so she started walking fast to catch up with them. As she did, the hawk angled toward her and circled overhead. Greta was glad to have its company.

Then suddenly the hawk dropped very low in the sky and flew toward her. Maybe it thinks I'm a mouse or some other animal hawks like to eat. What do I do now? Greta was frightened. She started running as fast as she could toward Claire and Jake, stumbling over sticks and pebbles.

Greta hadn't run very far when she looked up and saw a huge pair of claws coming toward her as the hawk dove with great speed. The next thing she knew she was high in the air.

Flapping its wings hard, the hawk had to make an effort to lift Greta's weight. At first Greta was too scared to think. Then she realized she had to calm down and figure

The hawk flew high

out a way to escape. I've always liked to fly, thought Greta, but not like this, dangling from the claws of a hungry hawk. I hope this is not the end of my life of adventure. I have to do something!

Greta yelled as loud as she could to the hawk, "I'm not a wild animal. I'm made of play fur and I'm not good to eat. Let me go!"

The hawk seemed annoyed by Greta's struggling, and began to peck at her. The hawk's beak hit Greta's backpack, which surely tasted terrible. With a furious squawk the hawk released Greta from its claws.

Happy to be free from the hawk's grip Greta thought, now I have another problem. I'm falling! Then she remembered her magic cape and reached behind her to unfold her red backpack. As the cape spread out behind her it slowed her fall and she glided safely to the ground.

Greta was so relieved to land that she forgot she was weak and tired. She ran fast all the way to the car and scrambled onto the seat just as Claire and Jake were climbing in.

"Gracious, you've gotten so muddy, little bear!" exclaimed Claire dusting off Greta's backpack.

You don't know the half of it, Greta thought. I just talked my way out of a very dangerous spot!

Claire and Jake began preparing a simple breakfast. Jake opened his pack and took out a box that said in green letters, "Crunchy Granola." He put some of the flakes in bowls with milk for him and Claire. It made a crunching sound as they chewed.

Greta decided to try some of it with honey. A bit of honey will restore my strength, she thought. She climbed in the pack and found the granola box and the honey jar. It took her a long time to clean her fur after the messy meal but it was worth it.

She remembered her flying cape

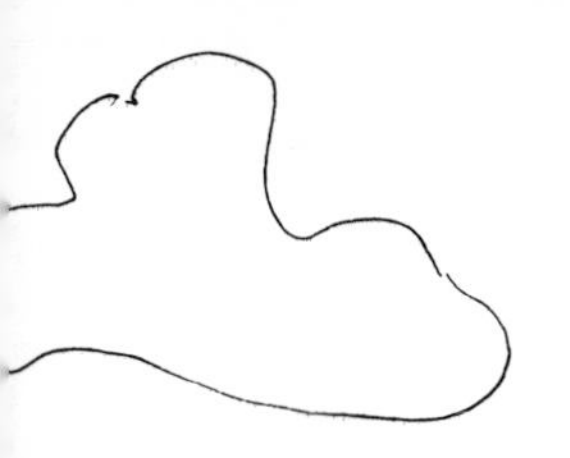

Upper Geyser Basin: Sapphire Pool; Mystic Falls; Morning Glory Pool; Riverside Geyser; Grotto Geyser; Giant Geyser; Grand Geyser;

Midway Geyser Basin: Excelsior Geyser Crater; Grand Prismatic Spring

Hoodoos

13
MORNING GLORY AND OLD FAITHFUL

After breakfast Jake took out a map, pointed to a spot and said, "Look, Claire, we're close to Old Faithful geyser. Let's pay it a visit."

Claire said, "I want to do a drawing of a geyser in my notebook."

Jake and Claire are good partners in the wilderness, Greta thought. What if I were with people who didn't enjoy watching elk or looking for geysers? I'm lucky I found such friends. They're also lucky they found a bear like me, of course.

As they drove along Greta saw a sign near a pine tree that said, "Upper Geyser Basin." Greta remembered this area from the guidebook. The geyser section of the book had had pictures of pools colored green, yellow, red and blue, surrounded by landscapes that looked like white sand. The book described how to drive to each geyser.

> Take the Grand Loop Road to Upper Geyser Basin and you will see many white cliffs, geysers and hot springs. Among the hot springs are Sapphire Pool, Jewel Geyser, Shell Geyser, Mustard Spring, Opalescent Pool, Spouter and Rainbow. Also in this area are stores, lodges and restaurants for visitors. Beyond the Black Sand Basin is the Old Faithful geyser which erupts approximately once an hour.

Lower Geyser Basin: Fountain Paint Pots; Great Fountain Geyser; White Dome Geyser

Mammoth Hot Springs: Minerva Terrace; Jupiter Terrace

Jake drove into the parking lot of the Old Faithful Visitor Center. Greta had heard a lot about Old Faithful geyser and how amazing its tall water spout was.

I don't see anything amazing spouting around here, she thought. There are a lot of people, though, more than I've seen since I left San Francisco.

Jake got out of the van to talk to a park ranger standing near the Visitor Center. Then he called to Claire, "The ranger says we just missed an eruption of Old Faithful and there won't be another one for about an hour. Let's make a quick visit to one of my favorite hot pools."

They drove a short distance and then climbed out of the car. Jake helped Claire on with her backpack and put Greta in it. They went toward the wooden walkways threaded around the geysers. Many people of all ages walked by looking at the pools. Greta thought it could take days to see all the geysers.

Castle Geyser was noisily spouting steam when they passed. Next they walked by Crested Pool which was near the river. Then Greta saw a pool more beautiful than any she could have imagined.

"Here we are," said Jake. "This is Morning Glory Pool."

The ground around the pool was mostly dry red gravel, but as it neared the edge of the pool it looked yellow. Then under a thin wisp of steam lay the bluest, brightest pool Greta had ever seen. You could see a deep hole in the center through the blue water. Greta tried to imagine how far down into the earth the hole went, and where it twisted and turned in its underground channels before it reached the sources of its water. Since the pool formed a circle in the ground with sides sloping toward the middle, and the water was a bright sky blue, the pool did indeed look like a giant Morning Glory blossom.

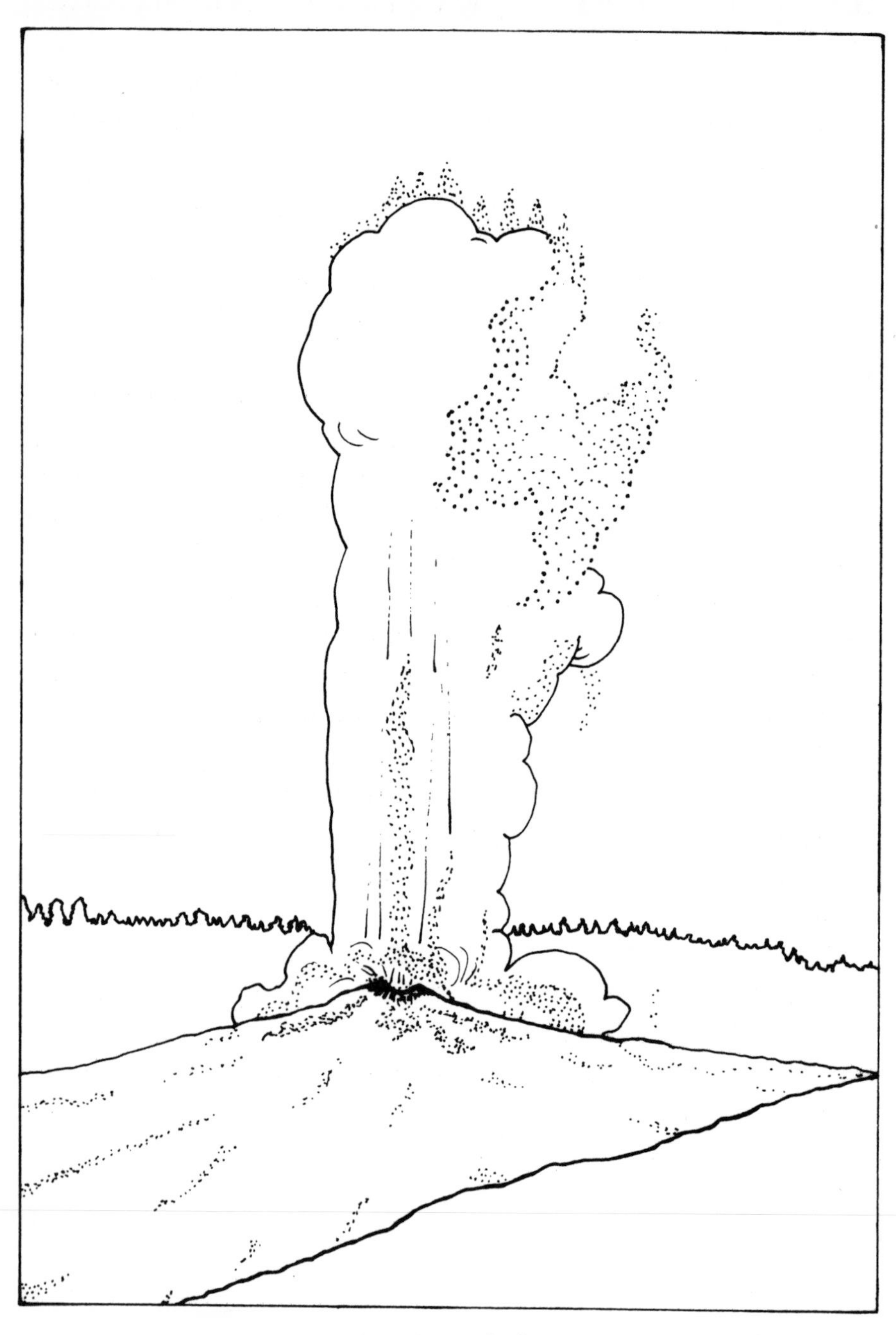

Old Faithful

One of the other tourists standing nearby did something that surprised Greta. He picked up a stone and threw it into the pool.

A ranger said to the man, "Don't throw anything into the pools, sir. If the hole of the geyser gets plugged up the flow of water is reduced; the pool will cool off and it will also gradually lose its beautiful colors."

I hope these pools never lose their beautiful colors, Greta thought. Jake and Claire turned and started walking back to the van to drive to Old Faithful.

Returning to the Visitor Center they saw many people near the geyser talking excitedly. Greta could see some water splashing over the rim of the crater. The splashes seemed to be getting bigger each time. Suddenly a huge column of water from the crater shot into the air.

The ranger next to Jake was named Rose. She whistled under her breath, "That's a big one. Over a hundred and thirty feet high!"

Greta thought the white water reaching to the sky and the sound it made as it sprayed into the air were very exciting. It made Greta want to jump up into the sunlight too.

Old Faithful had only been spouting a few minutes when the water column started to shrink. Like many wonderful adventures, this one passed quickly. Water droplets fell around the edges of the crater like rain, and the column shrank until all that was left of its magnificent height was steam boiling on the surface.

"I'd like to do a painting of Old Faithful," said Claire.

"Every eruption is different," said Ranger Rose, "and each one is beautiful."

"After many trips to Old Faithful, I never get tired of watching," said a man standing next to the ranger.

14

TROUT FISHING IN THE MADISON RIVER

Ranger Rose turned to introduce Jake and Claire to the man standing next to her. "I'd like you to meet my good friend, Charles." Charles shook hands with Jake and Claire. "Charles is an expert on the rivers of Yellowstone. He fishes here often."

"You're just the man I'd like to talk to," said Jake. "Where should I go fishing today?"

"There are a lot of good fishing spots in Yellowstone," said Charles, "but I'll tell you about my favorite. I love the section of the Madison River between Madison Junction and the park boundary. The water is excellent for dry-fly fishing. Dry-fly bait floats and you can watch it for signs of a fish biting. The stream is narrow enough in places that you can cast your fishing line clear across. These are great trout fishing waters. The hot springs warm the river so more plant life grows, and the bugs and fish eat like kings. It's so out of the way that nobody goes there. It's so peaceful that you can almost here the river singing as it flows along. You two should have a good time!"

"Sounds like what my city bones need," said Jake.

Sounds like what my city bones need too, thought Greta. I'd like to see the trout and hear the river sing.

"I hope you know," said the ranger, "that fishing in Yellowstone by people takes second place to fishing by animals. Some of the animals, such as bears and birds, fish for their food so the park service has rules to protect fish from dying out. People can only keep two fish of less than thirteen inches. Others have to be put back in the water. And I hope you have a fishing permit."

"Here's my permit," said Jake as he showed a small card to the ranger.

"Have a good time," said the ranger.

Jake and Claire walked back toward the van. Greta was getting sleepy in the midday sun. Claire put the pack on the car seat and Jake drove down the road toward Madison Junction. Greta decided this was her chance for a noon snooze. Bears need snoozes, she thought, as she curled up in the pack. When she closed her eyes pictures of colored fish appeared, and she fell asleep trying to imagine a trout.

Greta woke up when Jake pulled the van into a turnout at the side of the road. He stuck six poles into his backpack and he and Claire started down the slope. As they walked they saw some people fishing along the riverbank.

"You know, Claire," said Jake, "Maybe we should free the fish we catch today. We'll have a hard time keeping them fresh until tonight."

“Okay, but I need to practice anyway.” said Claire. “Someday when I’m camping I may really need to catch my food!”

After a while the river became narrow and quiet. Jake said, “Claire, this looks like the spot Charles was talking about.” They put their packs down on a rock.

What Greta had thought were several different fishing poles was really one that came to pieces so it was easy to carry. Jake screwed the three pieces of his fishing pole together to make one long fishing rod. Claire put her fishing rod together too. They strung clear line through the metal loops along the wooden rods. Jake pulled a tiny furry thing out of his pocket which Greta knew from her guidebook was a fake bug called a “fly.” Jake and Claire attached flies to the ends of their lines. A fly was made to look like a real bug so that hungry fish would try to swallow it. Inside the fly was a metal hook which would catch in the fish’s mouth. Then they could pull fish out of the water on the hooks. Jake and Claire began looking around for good places to stand along the river.

Jake picked a broad rock on which he could balance easily. He knew that fish often stayed near edges of rocks because the water is calmer there. Jake raised his fishing rod in one hand and shook it forward hard so that the clear line whirled out in the air across the river. Tossing out the fishing line was called "casting." As the end of the line touched the water Greta could see the fly dancing on the surface. Now and then Jake tugged on the fishing pole a little so the fly moved around in the water as if it were trying to swim. Claire did the same with her line watching the fly on the water.

After a few moments Claire's fly floated back in front of her. She pulled the line out of the water and started over. Several times she repeated this process. Greta liked to watch the line sail through the air and the fly float downstream. Everything seemed to move so slowly. Fishing made Greta feel peaceful.

Suddenly something tugged hard on Claire's line and she wound it in toward her. Greta could see a silvery fish on the end of the line, struggling to get loose. She thought it must feel uncomfortable to have a hook in its mouth. Claire pulled the fish toward the rock, bent over and reached into the water. Close up Greta could see that the fish had a coral colored belly, with spots on its sides and bright streaks of red under its mouth. Greta remembered from her guidebook that this was called a Cutthroat Trout and was native to the rivers of Yellowstone. Without taking the fish out of the water, because fish can only breathe in water, Claire took the hook out of its mouth and let it go. To Greta's surprise, the fish swam swiftly away!

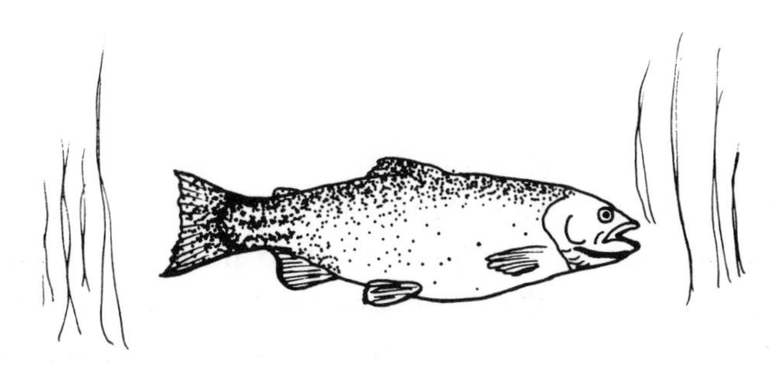

Yellowstone Cutthroat Trout

"Which side of a fish has the most scales?" asked Claire.

"I don't know," said Jake.

"The outside," said Claire.

"Ug," said Jake.

"You know, I bet I could do a beautiful painting of a trout."

"I hope the painting's better than the joke," laughed Jake.

Jake and Claire pulled their lines out of the water and walked down the riverbank looking for new places to fish.

"Look at the frogs, Jake!" said Claire as they passed several small green animals hopping on rocks in the shallow water.

Greta watched the figures of her two friends grow smaller as they walked on downstream. Left alone by the river, Greta listened to the songs of the birds. She stretched out all four legs and soaked up the sun's heat.

Then Greta saw a big white bird with a long graceful neck moving on top of the water. Out of the tall grasses along the riverbank came another big one with two little ones swimming behind. From pictures in the guidebook Greta recognized the beautiful birds as swans. They swam downstream, stopping occasionally to dip their heads, stick their tails in the air and search underwater for tasty bugs and grasses. Greta watched until they swam out of sight around a bend in the river. Then she dozed in the sun.

After awhile Claire came back alone to the rock where Greta was stretched out. "Looks as though you have a great spot for an afternoon daydream," said Claire as she lay down on the riverbank and closed her eyes.

Awhile later Jake walked up. "Ready to head back now, Claire?" he asked.

"Sure, slow poke," said Claire. She put Greta in her pack and slung it on her back. She and Jake started walking back through the meadow.

"Did you like trout fishing?" asked Jake.

"Does a bear sleep in the woods?" said Claire.

Out of the tall reeds came the swans

15
PANIC AT PICNIC POINT

Back at the van Claire said, "Let's eat our lunch outside. It's such a warm day."

They took sandwiches, drinks and cookies and spread them out on a wooden table under a tree. Claire put her backpack down on a moss covered mound nearby. Groups of people were eating at other tables in the picnic area.

"What's white on the outside, green on the inside and hops?" asked Claire.

"I don't know, but I bet you're going to tell me," said Jake.

"A frog sandwich."

"Well, we only have lettuce and tomato today."

"How boring," said Claire.

On her comfortable mossy spot Greta was enjoying the breeze and a little honey. Suddenly she was thrown high into the air! Landing Greta discovered that four children from one of the picnicking families had decided to play catch with her.

They don't even know the difference between bears and balls, she thought. Help! Where's Claire?

The children playing hide and seek ran deep into the forest out of sight of the picnic tables. After awhile they reached a meadow and collapsed laughing in the grass. One of them had a candy bar and the kids shared it and

talked about running away together to live in the woods. When they finished eating they tossed the candy wrapper in the grass. I don't like being in the woods, Greta thought, with people who mess up the animals' home.

Two of the boys started playing tag. Running fast, the smaller boy slipped on a log and fell down hard. He cried, "I've hurt my leg!"

"I've hurt my leg!"

"We'd better go back to the car now," said one of them. They got up together helping their injured friend walk. Then they stopped in silence. "I don't know the way back," one said.

"We're lost," said his friend. She hugged Greta tight and started to cry. "We'll freeze and be eaten by wild beasts. We don't have any water. And we'll starve."

What a way to end my career as an adventurer, thought Greta.

One little girl said, "We've got to be brave and sensible. Let's try to remember how we came here. We should save our voices to yell for help. Maybe someone will hear us. Stick together and yell for help."

The children started walking toward the stream yelling, "Help! We're lost. Come find us. Help!"

The children were headed the wrong way. Greta Bear tumbled out of the little girl's arms and rolled in the direction of the forest. The girl ran to pick her up and the others followed. Good, thought Greta, I know this is the way back. They walked through the forest for what felt like a long time. Then suddenly Greta saw Jake coming toward them. All the children shrieked for joy and ran over to him.

Jake hugged them but also said sternly, "Well, my friends, you're lucky to be found. People should never walk into a forest they don't know without a guide or a compass. At least you hadn't gone very far and I could hear you from the picnic ground. Otherwise the situation could have been grim. From now on don't wander off until you know a lot more about making your way in the wilderness. Now follow me." The children silently followed Jake back to the picnic ground.

When they saw their parents the children ran to them. The girl carrying Greta dropped her in her excitement. Everyone hugged and kissed in their relief. The children thanked Jake for rescuing them.

Claire found Greta at the edge of the woods, covered with dust. "There you are, Greta Bear. I'm so glad to see you back. I wondered what happened to you. You've had a rough afternoon. Let's go clean you off."

Those kinds of adventures, thought Greta, I can do without.

"You've had a rough afternoon," said Claire

16

YELLOWSTONE'S VERY OWN GRAND CANYON

After dusting off Greta and straightening her backpack, Claire and Jake got into the van. As they drove through the park, Greta relaxed and saw many interesting things out the window. She was becoming quite good at identifying animals at a distance. Now when she saw a moose she wasn't afraid. And she wasn't startled when she saw an elk.

She was beginning to be able to identify the birds as they flew across the sky. On the river she had seen the huge white shape of an osprey sitting high up in a tree near its nest. In the marshes where the moose grazed flocks of black and gray Canada geese announced themselves by their noisy honking. Sometimes Greta even saw pelicans, with their big yellow beaks for carrying fish, swimming down the river with the swans.

Greta could recognize her favorite meadows and rivers by their shapes and colors and by the way the mountains looked rising behind them. She now understood that it would be possible to live in the great outdoors and be very happy. They passed signs as they drove along: Terrace Spring, Gibbon River Falls, Virginia Cascades, Artist Point, Grand Canyon.

Grand Canyon? Greta thought the Grand Canyon was in Arizona. Jake turned off the main road. At a small sign that read, "Trail," he parked the car and he and Claire started rummaging around in the back of the truck, gathering clothes and gear. What next, Greta thought?

Jake and Claire took off their sneakers and put on hiking boots. They changed into beige shorts made of strong material like canvas. All their clothes looked very comfortable because they were made specially for use in the great outdoors. Jake emptied everything out of his pack except a plastic jar of water, a bag of nuts, several apples and a cotton scarf. He pulled the lightweight pack onto his back. Claire put on hers and they began walking down a narrow trail into the woods.

From the pocket in Claire's pack, Greta could see over her shoulder and down the path. The trees along the trail were pines and their needles made the forest smell delicious. The dry ground on the path had been worn to a sandy powder by the feet of many hikers. Now and then to the side of the trail Greta saw chipmunks and squirrels busily eating or running across logs. Gradually the path wound uphill.

Suddenly the woods cleared on their right and Greta saw an amazing landscape. Beyond the edge of the cliff the earth opened into a huge chasm. This surely must be the Grand Canyon of Yellowstone!

The steep walls sank hundreds of feet to the bottom of the canyon where a big river rushed through. Where they stood on the cliff the earth was as yellow as if the rocks had been dusted with pale chalk. The rushing sound of the river bounced up the walls of the canyon to the trail.

Birds soared through the wide open space of the canyon. Seeing this made Greta want to fly too. She thought how wonderful it must feel to look out at such a big space and be able to leave the edge of the cliff to soar into the wind above the river.

None of them standing on the cliff had wings so they continued down the trail on foot. Then Jake came to a place where the trail made a sharp turn. From here Greta could see a sparkling waterfall in the distance spilling down to the canyon floor where it rolled into the river. Claire and Jake began walking down the steep trail.

At least "walking" was the only word Greta knew for it, but it certainly was a peculiar way of walking. Jake and Claire kind of hopped and slid in the dirt. They would each put a foot forward and dig into the hill with the sides of their shoes, making small indentations in the hillside as they went. After awhile Greta got used to the motion and it felt a little bit like dancing, dancing with the hill.

All at once Claire slipped on some loose dirt and when her foot hit a rock she stumbled over it. This jolted Greta out of the pack and onto the dirt. Claire was so focused on hiking that she didn't notice Greta's fall.

Sitting on the ground, Greta thought, what do I do now?

As Jake and Claire disappeared down the hillside, Greta grew braver. I'll follow them into the canyon. Surprises and accidents are part of adventure, she thought. Besides, they might not come back up this way, and I better get going if I don't want to spend the night here!

Greta dusted off her fur, stood up on her hind paws and started walking down the hill toward the small dots that were all she could now see of Claire and Jake. To her surprise her feet wobbled and slipped on the loose gravel. Then she remembered how Claire and Jake had walked and decided to try it.

She bent her knees and placed one paw firmly a few inches down the hillside. When the dirt began to slide under her feet she kept her legs steady. To her satisfaction the forward foot lodged in the dirt and the sliding stopped after a moment. She tried using this motion with the next paw. Then the next. Gradually she quickened her pace.

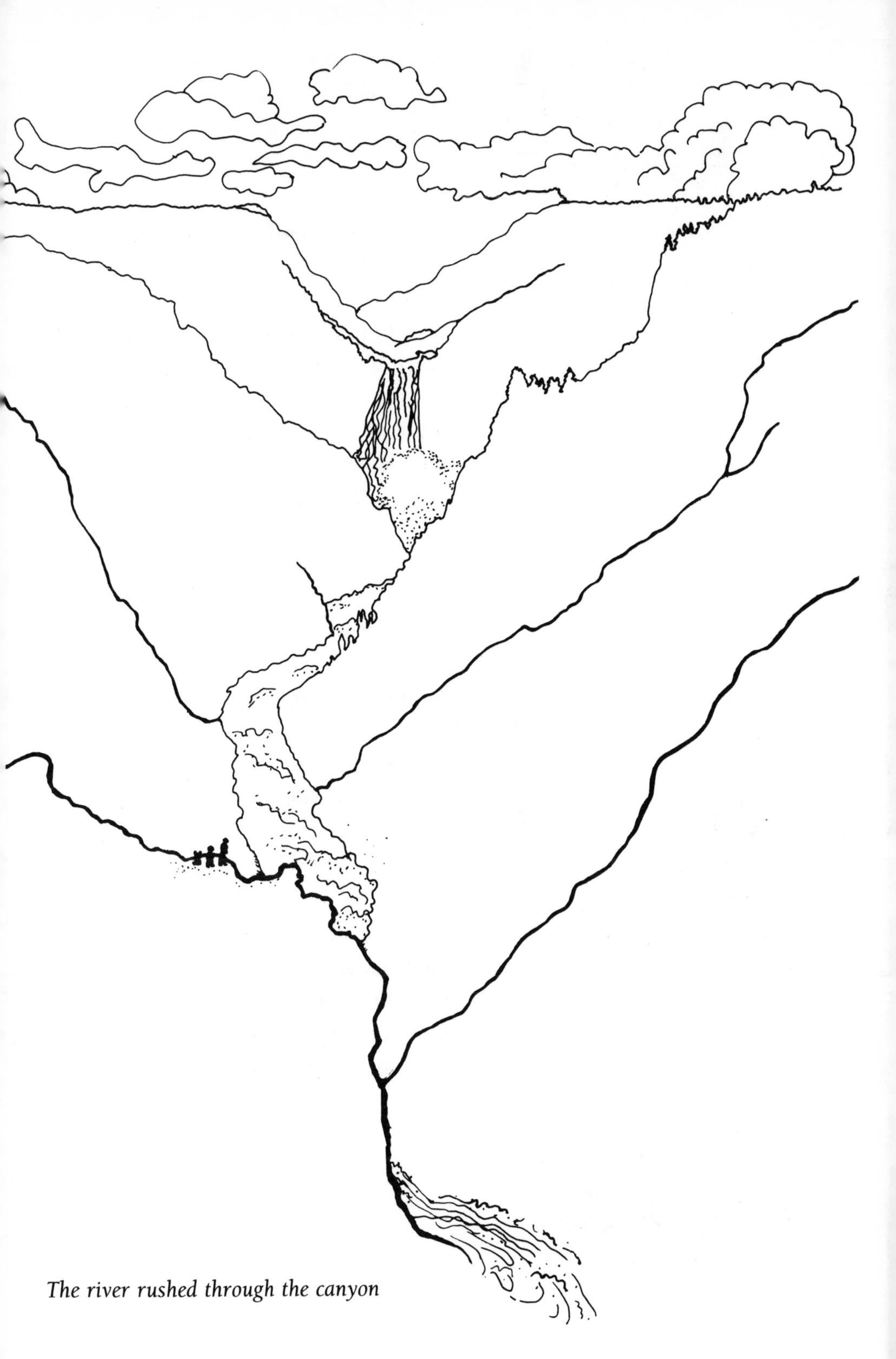

The river rushed through the canyon

Mountain Goat

After a spell of sliding and stopping she saw that the special way Claire had slid had made it possible for her to move quickly downhill without falling. She noticed too that when she relaxed, her breathing moved rhythmically with her walking. Now, she thought, is a good time for a hiking song:

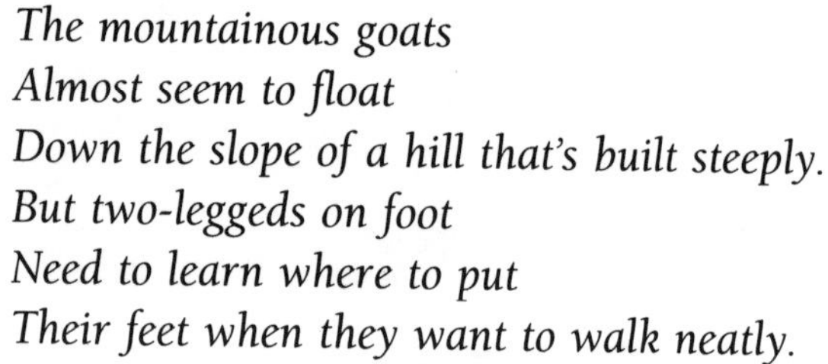

The mountainous goats
Almost seem to float
Down the slope of a hill that's built steeply.
But two-leggeds on foot
Need to learn where to put
Their feet when they want to walk neatly.

Marmot

Oh, canyon squirrels and marmots
Simply don't give a thought
Hopping around to their liking.
But two-leggeds may slide
Downhill by backsides
Unless they practice their hiking.

Ground Squirrel

The song helped Greta keep her rhythm as she moved down the hill. Soon she began to catch up with Claire and Jake and as they reached the bottom of the canyon she was right behind them. Although it didn't necessarily start out that way, hiking was fun when you learned how, Greta decided. Now they were at Yellowstone River.

And what a river it was! Bigger than the Madison, and faster. The water rushed by in white waves over the rocks and made a roaring sound that blew up the sides of the canyon on the wind. Greta could hear pebbles grating as they were dragged downstream by the current.

From where Greta, Claire and Jake stood on the riverbank, the color of the river in the canyon seemed very special. Where it wasn't foamy white the water appeared to be a deep emerald green. Greta thought this must be the most beautiful river in the world. Certainly it was the most beautiful one she had ever seen.

Jake and Claire put their packs down on the ground and started walking on the big rocks along the riverbank. Greta knew they would be coming back for their packs. She climbed on top of Claire's to rest after what had been a long hike for a right size bear.

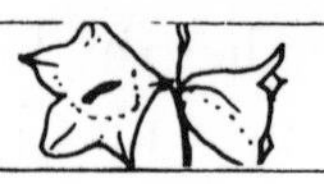

17
PIKAS ON ROCKS

Greta heard something scrambling and looked to see what it was. Up the hill she noticed a small brown animal with round ears and bright eyes. It was bigger than a mouse and smaller than a rabbit, and was running back and forth on the rocks. It was carrying bunches of blue flowers in its mouth to a sunny spot and dumping them there. Again and again the animal disappeared from sight to return with a fresh load of leaves and flowers. Some of the plants on the rocks were drying out in the sun and turning yellow.

As Greta twisted around to get a better look, her paw knocked a pebble loose and the animal sat up quickly. When the animal saw Greta Bear it let out a long squeak. At the sound of the squeak another animal just like the first appeared from a crack between two rocks some distance away. They sat upright staring at Greta.

"I'm only a toy bear," said Greta. "I won't hurt you. Come talk to me."

When Greta spoke, at first the animals scurried under their rocks to hide. Then they cautiously stuck their heads out. One said, "Aren't you a rather small bear?"

"I'm just the right size for me," said Greta. "And I'm not like most bears you see in the forest. I have soft white stuffing inside of me. I'm just learning to be wild. Who are you?"

A small animal appeared from a crack in the rocks

“We are pikas,” said the animals. “We live in the rocks. We’re making hay to eat in the winter when fresh plants are hard to find.” One of the pikas looked at the other and said, “Let’s go and visit with the small bear, okay?” Then they scrambled down the piles of rocks.

I like these animals, Greta thought. They are nervous, but they’re friendly, and brave enough to come talk to me. Also they are quite a nice size for wild animals.

The two pikas ran up and sat in front of Greta sniffing and wiggling their whiskers. When they were standing next to Greta she saw they were nearly the same size as she was.

“Where did you come from? Are you going to stay here? Is your stuffing made of milkweed or rabbit’s hair?”

They asked lots of questions very fast all at once and didn’t give Greta time to answer.

“Why don’t you come play with us?” said the pikas. “We can go running on our favorite rockslide.”

Pika on rocks

They climbed up the steep wall

"Thank you, but I must wait here for my friends, Jake and Claire. They are walking down the riverbank. But soon they'll be back." Greta liked talking to the pikas, but she'd had enough rocksliding today.

"Good to meet you, stuffed bear," said the pikas in unison. "We've got to be going. We have a lot to do before the sun goes down. Come back and see us again." They scurried up the hillside.

They certainly are busy animals, Greta thought. Not like bears who appreciate sitting still. She dug an apple and some nuts out of the pack for her afternoon snack. The water in the thermos refreshed her after the long hike. Then she sat quietly gazing at the emerald water catching the sunlight and carrying it downstream. When Jake and Claire returned, Greta was asleep by the river.

"Well, little bear, looks as though you've fallen out of your pack," Claire said. "Hey, Jake, let's hike up a different route than we came down."

Greta woke up at the sound of Claire's voice. It's a good thing I'm an observant bear, Greta thought, and watched you hiking down the canyon. Otherwise we might never have found each other again.

Claire put Greta in the pack, lifted it on her back, and she and Jake started climbing up the trail out of the canyon.

18
WILD BEARS

After a long hike to the top of the canyon Jake and Claire turned around for a parting look. Greta could hardly believe they had hiked so far. A good feeling of new accomplishment swelled in her chest. Here in Yellowstone she was learning exciting things about the great outdoors, and about herself. I can do more than I thought I could and I feel ready for any adventure. I certainly am a remarkable bear!

Greta watched the afternoon light filtering through the trees as Claire and Jake headed down the trail. Jake's footstep cracked a branch lying in the dirt, and the sound startled Greta out of her thoughts. The sound apparently startled something else. They heard rustling in the woods and a low growl. When Greta looked in the direction of the sounds she saw something she had dreamed of–wild bears! Some distance away were two cubs rolling over each other in the grass. Close to them was a huge brown mother bear. She had been nosing for roots in the earth and looked up.

Jake and Claire instantly froze on the path when they saw the bears. Greta became very still and watched to see what the bears would do next. The mother bear made a deep grunt; at this signal the cubs immediately stopped playing and scurried up the nearest tree. Jake and Claire

A low growl came from nearby

The cubs scurried up the trees

were now very slowly walking down the trail in the opposite direction from the cubs.

Greta could feel that Claire and Jake were frightened. And the mother bear was protective of her cubs; she thought that people might want to harm them. The huge bear growled and moved menacingly toward them.

I've got to do something fast, thought Greta. Then she remembered a sound that Ursa Major had taught her which bears understood meant you were their friend. Greta let out a long low humming sound.

When the mother bear heard the humming she stopped short, paused, then turned around and loped away down the hill. Claire, her eyes wide, turned to look over her shoulder at Greta Bear. Then Claire looked back down the trail, and she and Jake began walking quickly in the direction of the parking lot.

Greta realized that they had been in great danger. The mother bear might have attacked to protect the cubs or her territory. But since the mother bear hadn't followed them they were beginning to breathe easily again, though they kept walking.

Through the trees Greta could see the outline of the parking lot. She felt happy when they finally reached the clearing. They sat down on some rocks. Jake took off his pack, wiped his forehead with his scarf and let out a long sigh of relief. He and Claire both stayed awhile silently, thinking of what had just happened.

Safe now, Greta could enjoy her memory of the bears. The cubs were a cinnamon color and had played with each other rolling and swatting like puppies. The mother bear was so big and powerful that when she moved, Greta felt as though part of the hillside were taking a step. Greta was glad to have seen wild bears at least once in her life. If wild bears wanted to be left alone, she hoped people wouldn't bother them or invade their territory.

"There's the Indian ranger, Hawk," Jake said. "I'm going over there to tell him about the bears we saw."

Claire stayed on the rock with Greta Bear. "Oh, Greta," she said. "I knew you were special but I didn't know you were magic! And I didn't know you could speak to wild bears!"

"I'm a friend of all bears," said Greta, "and, of course, bears are friends of all other animals too. I'll sing you a song about wild bears."

The bears heard the humming

When you meet a bear
You see fuzzy brown hair
And think it looks like your teddy,
Be careful, beware
If you don't take care
Bears may do things for which you're not ready.
Grumbiddy dum, O grumbiddy dum,
Bears may do things for which you're not ready.

They're quite long in their length
And they don't know their strength
So think twice of accepting a bear hug;
They're not sure you're their friend
For some people tend
To think they'd look cuter as bear rugs.
Grumbiddy dum, O grumbiddy dum,
To think they'd look cuter as bear rugs.

Be quite understanding
No feeding or handling
Walk slowly the other direction.
If bears see you come
Most especially don't run
Playing catch is the idea of bear fun.
Grumbiddy dum, O grumbiddy dum,
Playing catch is the idea of bear fun.

If you love wild bears
Help the parks remain theirs
Don't disturb all the places the bears roam.
Keep in mind your bear shoulds
For when you're in the woods
You're surely a guest in a bear's home.
Grumbiddy dum, O grumbiddy dum,
You're surely a guest in a bear's home.

"What a great song, Greta," said Claire. "We should have a club for people who love bears and want to help them live happily in forests. How about it, Greta?"

"We can call it Friends of Bears," said Greta, "and the club signal is a bear hug."

"That's it!" said Claire, and gave Greta a big hug.

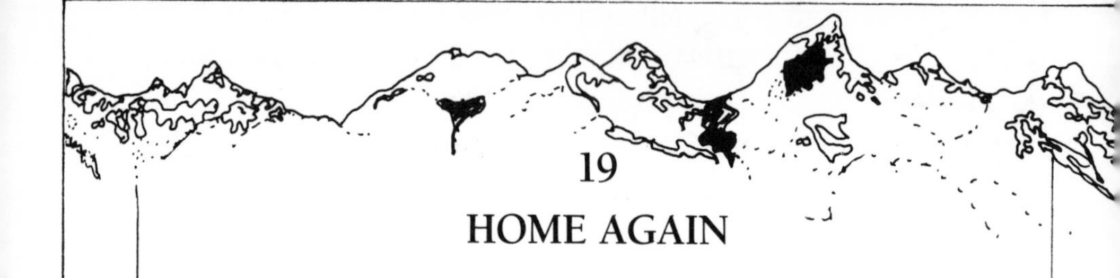

19
HOME AGAIN

Jake came walking back to where Claire and Greta Bear were sitting. They climbed into the van and drove out of the woods onto the main road. As they went Claire painted a picture of bear cubs in her sketchbook which by now had many drawings of animals and plants they had seen.

"Greta's a very special bear, Jake," Claire said.

"I know you think so," said Jake.

"You would too, if you knew what I know," said Claire smiling.

Meeting wild bears makes me hungry, Greta thought. She burrowed deep into Claire's pack until she found the honey jar, took the top off, and put both paws into the lovely golden syrup. When a little honey spilled, she wiped it up with a scarf as carefully as she could. Some granola bits fell between the apples, and then tumbled deeper into the pack. Greta nudged the granola bits and watched them slide down the slippery water jar. She pushed them toward the honey pot to see how far they would roll before they got stuck.

After awhile, Greta began wondering where they were. She crawled up to look around. The afternoon had become a dark blue evening and the air had cooled.

"Well, my friend," said Jake to Claire,

"I think it's time to leave Yellowstone and head back to Jackson Hole. I've sure had a good time showing you the park. If you want to come with me sometime we can visit another national park. Or we could come back here. I always have work here photographing animals, and you are fine company in the wilderness. Shall we visit Yellowstone together again?"

"Does a goose honk? Does a swan swim? Does a bear sleep in the woods?" answered Claire.

Jake laughed and hugged Claire. They would both remember the special, warm time they'd shared on this trip.

"Greta," said Claire, "we have to leave Yellowstone. Now I'd like to take you to my home."

I'm sure your home is nice, thought Greta, but I think leaving the park is a terrible idea! I'm just beginning to learn about Yellowstone's adventures. The guidebook says that there are many more animals here we didn't see—big horn sheep, mule deer, coyotes and antelope. And what about boating on Yellowstone Lake? Perhaps we should stay until the snow begins to fall so we can learn to ski. I can't imagine why anyone would want to leave Yellowstone Park! Greta went on thinking about the reasons they should stay, at least for one more day.

Then Greta thought about running away from Claire and Jake. They want to go back to Jackson Hole; that sounds like a city, she thought. And I want to be wild. I'll join the wild animals! But I've come to love Claire now, she thought. I like travelling with her and Jake. I already gave up one friend to go wild, she thought, remembering the floppy moose.

Greta thought over her belief that she was an adventurous bear. She decided that if this were true, she could find adventure wherever she went, even outside the borders of Yellowstone. Maybe wild is something I can carry with me even in the city, she thought. This cheered her up. Perhaps this new place will be exciting too. But, thought Greta, Jackson Hole is a funny name for an exciting place.

Greta was getting tired and she lay down so she could think more easily. After a few minutes she fell asleep.

When she woke up they were still driving, but now Greta saw stars shining outside. In the moonlight she could tell that instead of pine forests there were wide flat fields on either side of the road. In them were the dark shapes of haystacks. Jake drove on and on. After several hours the landscape became hilly again, then mountainous.

Now Greta could see a pointed line of mountains with snowy tops in the distance. There were houses built on the flat land in the valley. Jake turned off the main road. At the end of the driveway he parked near a log cabin surrounded by pine trees. The lights in the windows made the house look cozy and inviting.

Jake and Claire climbed out of the car carrying several bundles, including Greta in the pack. When they knocked at the door a dark-haired woman opened it. She broke into a big smile when she saw her son and daughter. "Welcome back to Jackson Hole," she said to Jake. "And welcome home to you!" she said as she hugged Claire.

"Mommy, you won't believe all the things that happened to me and Jake and my new bear, Greta." When Claire leaned over to put her pack down, she noticed granola sticking on the zipper and

A hungry bear

pockets. "What a mess," Claire said. "The top must have come off the honey jar. It spilled all over my pack. But at least the bear is clean. How do you like my new bear, Mommy? Greta shared all my adventures with me in Yellowstone. She went everywhere with us. I made a notebook of drawings of the animals we saw. You know, Greta even got stolen once and found me again. Then she saved us from a fire and wild bears! And we're all going camping together again soon!" In her excitement Claire almost forgot to give her mother a big hug. But now in her arms, she felt safe and happy and suddenly sleepy.

"That sounds exciting for another day," said Claire's mother. "But tonight it's time for Claire and Wonder Bear to go to bed!"

Wonder Bear, thought Greta, I like that.

"Goodnight, my friend," said Jake as he gave Claire a kiss.

"I am kind of sleepy," said Claire as she walked into her bedroom. Her mother tucked Claire and Greta under a soft quilt.

Under a quilt is a fine place for an adventurer to end a day in the great outdoors, thought Greta. You know, now I think I understand what Ursa meant when she said that love is magic. When Claire and Jake and I love each other and are friends, we are freer and more powerful than we ever were alone. I bet even more exciting adventures will open up to us now. Jake and Claire are such fine friends of bears. How I hope we'll see Yellowstone together again.

Ah, Yellowstone, thought Greta. I wonder where the wild animals are tonight? Are the swans in their nests? Are the elk on their pine mats? Are the spotted trout floating in the emerald river, and the wild bears rolled up in their cozy dens under the stars?

Greta Bear looked outside and saw Ursa Major shining in the sky. Greta climbed out of bed and sat on the sill of the open window. "Ursa," she said, "how can I get back to Yellowstone?"

"You can see the animals anytime you want," Ursa said in a soft voice. "Your adventures have just begun. You will meet many friends of bears. And your flying cape will take you wherever you wish."

"And if I meet more danger how will I know what to do?" asked Greta.

"Here's a heart. Just follow it!" said Ursa Major, and she sent a soft red heart on a trail of stardust to Greta Bear.

Greta placed the heart on her chest and felt at peace. She climbed back under Claire's warm quilt. From high in the sky Ursa Major sang her to sweet adventurous sleep with the bear's lullaby:

Whose dreams are so sweet
As a bear's dreams?
Whose feet are so soft
As a bear's paws?

Whose nose is so close
To the eyes that are closed
Dreaming the dreams
That my bear dreams?

O sun on the waves
O green speckled trout
Swim in the dreams
That my bear dreams.

White stars flying high
O moon hanging low
Shine in the dreams
That my bear dreams.

A heart as strong
As a bear's heart
A hug as warm
As a bear's hug
A love burning bright
As the stars in the night
These are the dreams
That my bear dreams.

"Here's a heart. Just follow it!" said Ursa Major

A BEAR'S LULLABY

When you finish this book
you become a member of

FRIENDS OF BEARS CLUB

and you can receive your complimentary membership card, stickers and newsletter by sending a postcard with your name and address plus Zip code to:

Greta Bear Enterprizes
Post Office Box 9525
Berkeley, California 94709 U.S.A.

GRETA BEAR WELCOMES YOU
TO
FRIENDS OF BEARS!